NORMAN FIRTH

---◆---

COLIN'S GHOST

Complete and Unabridged

LINFORD
Leicester

First published in Great Britain

First Linford Edition
published 2019

A catalogue record for this book is available
from the British Library.

ISBN 978–1–4448–3983–8

Published by
F. A. Thorpe (Publishing)
Anstey, Leicestershire

Set by Words & Graphics Ltd.
Anstey, Leicestershire
Printed and bound in Great Britain by
T. J. International Ltd., Padstow, Cornwall

This book is printed on acid-free paper

Colin's Ghost

1

Gold of the Incas

On the high top of a plateau, verdant and treacherous, in the age-old, uncharted jungle of Peru, two men hacked their way through the green Hell.

Their bearers had fled the night before; even their guide had gone. For they were nearing the lost, forbidden city of Kosan.

Globules of sweat stood out upon their faces; the haversacks on their backs seemed to weigh them down towards the hot clamminess of the swampy ground they were traveling on; multi-coloured parakeets made the hazy atmosphere hideous with raucous cries, and often a long, treacherous snake would unfold before them and glide away into the thickness of the trees.

Arthur Birnes paused in his trail-cutting, mopped his brow, pulled the wet stickiness of his khaki shirt away from his chest, and groaned.

'Hell, Colin,' he said dismally. 'Let's turn back. God knows where we'll wind up if we keep going — and at least we stand a fair chance of getting back from here.'

Colin Davis shook his head, stubbornly.

'You can turn back, Arthur,' he told the other man, 'but I'm keeping on. We can't be far away now. The natives deserted, and that means we're at least in the forbidden territory. Can't you feel something in the air? Something they felt?'

Birnes stood silent, listening. The calls of the parakeets had died away now; the chatter of the monkeys seemed to come from far off. In this fringe of the jungle where they stood, a great and unreal silence lay over everything as if all within that section was dead, lifeless, and long forgotten. It filled Birnes with nameless fear — of *what*, he could not tell. He said, uneasily:

'Yes, I can feel something — something strange. And I don't like it. It's as if — as if we're trespassing on dangerous ground.'

4

Colin laughed, smoothed his fair hair back under his helmet, and shouldered his haversack again.

'Come on, let's get along. Don't give up now, Arthur.'

Birnes nodded, but his face remained uneasy as he followed his companion again. It could hardly have been ten minutes before they burst from the trees, at the extreme edge of the plateau, and looked down into a valley surrounded by high mountain ranges — gazed down on the dead city of Kosan!

Dead was the word for it exactly.

It lay far below, under a shimmering blanket of heat; it looked almost like a mirage, wavering and rippling before their eyes. The outer part was derelict and ruined, murdered by the encroaching jungle; but the centre of the city stood as firm and bold as in the days long past when it had been populated by a teeming, copper-hued people, working and laughing and loving amongst its statuesque buildings and wide streets.

And since those days no human being had ever strode along past those tall white houses, through the long rectangular courtyards wherein stood dried-up fountains of exquisite design. It was indeed a city without life; and strangely enough there was no sign of animals within it. A solemn, brooding stillness held the reins of time.

Colin and Arthur stood rooted; they had hoped for some momentous discovery, but nothing as magnificent as this. This was a dream city of gold and gems; even from that distance they could see the dull glowing of burnished gold which had been used in the construction of many of the buildings. What had driven the people away — or wiped them out so completely?

They ran over in their minds what they had heard of the lost city. It was little enough, and their expedition had been based on practically nothing but myth and legend and a few native stories. A branch of the Incas had wandered far inland, to escape their cruel ruler; they had founded a city in a pleasant valley, which had grown and prospered for long after the original Inca Empire was wiped out. Here, they were safe and secure.

And yet — something had happened to eliminate them completely.

Native legend did not attempt to describe what; those who had seen the city had been too afraid and superstitious to venture into its heart. They knew only that it was a dead city, and evil.

Minutes had passed; now Colin gave a shaky laugh and said, 'Well? Glad we kept going now? Think of the contribution we'll make to history!'

'Damn history,' grunted Birnes. 'We'll be rich! You aren't trying to tell me you'd be fool enough to let anyone else in on this, are you?'

Colin looked surprised, but nodded. 'Of course, that's the main idea. We can take a few trinkets for ourselves, but the important point is to find out what happened to these people and their civilisation.'

Birnes said: 'Is it? I'm of a different opinion, Colin. I vote we keep our mouths shut, get back to civilisation, and fit out an expedition to come back and collect as much of this stuff here as we can carry. Damn it all, why give all this to the Government after the trouble we've taken to find it?'

'Don't be an idiot, Arthur. We can carry enough away with us as will make us rich for life. What more do we need?'

'No!' It was a savage exclamation, and Colin looked uneasily at the other man. 'No. Why content ourselves with a few odds and ends when it's all ours?'

'Now look here, Arthur, let's get one or two things cleared up before we go any further. In the first place *I* organized and paid for this expedition. I asked you along because you were down on your luck, and — I don't like to remind you of it — but I'm paying you for your services. I'm not unwilling for you to take whatever you can carry away with you, but the main reason for the expedition was to make our findings known to science. And that's exactly what I propose to do. If you don't like the idea, I'm sorry . . . but I'm going through with it.'

Birnes scowled, and turned away to hide the glitter in his eyes. He was a weak man, and the sight of those gold-encrusted buildings had destroyed his self-control completely. He wanted to keep the secret of this place, to share it with no one.

Colin laughed suddenly, said: 'Let's not quarrel now, Arthur. Let's push on and see what we can find out.'

Birnes nodded, and twisting his features into a contrite expression he said: 'I'm sorry, Colin. Forget what I said. Don't know what could have come over me — just lost myself for a minute.'

'Forget it. Let's get on.'

Fifteen minutes saw them traversing the undergrowth-bound paths of the outer city; ten minutes later they drew clear of the jungle-ridden patch, and stood in a wide square, gazing with awed eyes at the majestic temple before them. There was a well in the courtyard, which had once been used for human sacrifice, but was now silent and waterless. They passed this grisly relic, approached the semi-open doors of the temple itself. A feeling that they were going to see something stunning in its tragedy came over them, and they halted before edging through the massive, gold-sheeted doors.

Then they were inside, and their eyes were gradually becoming accustomed to the gloom.

In the dim light from a circular hole in the roof, a grim scene was presented to them.

They were in the temple which had probably been erected to a sun god. Upon a stone altar at the far end lay a heap of small bones in the shape of a skeleton; buried amongst them was a long-handled, wonderfully carved knife. A second, larger skeleton lay to the right of the altar, a gold head-dress beside it.

And then their gaze covered the rest of that vast room. Dry, collapsed skeletons, heaps of bones; bones which had once been men and women in horribly contorted positions; brittle bones which crunched sickeningly underfoot as they pressed towards the altar.

The temple of the dead, in the city of the dead. The whole place was crammed with those rotting reminders of the people who had suffered some unimaginable fate. And the answer lay beside the altar, in a rolled gold tube, clutched in the hand of the skeleton who had obviously been their High Priest.

Colin took the tube and read the stiff piece of skin which he extracted from the inside. It had been specially treated, and was perfectly preserved. Arthur said, eagerly: 'Can you read it?'

Colin nodded, and there, in that temple, by the light from the opening high above, he began to read:

"Written by Fe-non, Scribe to the High Priest of Kosan, in the Temple of the Sun, fifty thousand moons after the founding of our city, our people lie dead and dying; our race must perish.

"This, because of the mysterious plague which has struck upon us, smiting us down in our thousands in the street, in our homes. We know not the nature of this plague, save that men swell up in agony under it, and die most horribly. Nor can we relieve them. At first we thought it would pass, and threw its victims into the ceremonial burial pit in the main square. Only when we were reduced from fifty thousand to three thousand or less, did we realise that there was to be no cessation until death had claimed us all.

"'Those of us who remained flocked to the temple, for the plague was killing tens by the minute. For five days and nights our High Priest sacrificed young virginal maids, while I penned this at his dictation. It was of no avail; he himself died while executing a sacrifice.

"'And now there are but fifty of us left, who too must die. Many have left the city, hoping to return to our ancestors' country, if it still remains, but there is little hope that these will reach their destination. They will perish miserably in the jungle, prey of the beasts which roam there.

"'I, Fe-non, leave this scroll for those who come after, that the last days of our great people should be recorded. I must put aside my work, now; the plague swells my hand so that it is agony to write.'"

That was all there was to it; and Colin remained silent for long minutes when he had read the final word.

Birnes was jittery; he said: 'Hell, d'you suppose it's — it's catching?'

'There's no danger, if my guess is right,' said Colin. 'I see it this way: these people, according to this scroll, neither buried nor burnt their dead. Seemingly, with their split from the main body of Incas, they developed customs of their own, one of which was to throw their dead into a ceremonial pit. Over a period of years that was bound to cause something in the nature of a disease. But the poor devils didn't realise it at all. Probably the pit was deep in the first place, and no effect was experienced. But as time went on and the pit filled up, the plague was caused. Naturally, after the passage of all this time, the bodies are all skeletons, therefore the plague is no longer virulent. I think you'll find we'll be all right, Arthur.'

Reassured, they started out to explore the rest of the temple. The wonders they found held them entranced until they noticed, with a shock, that the sun was already low against the hills.

Birnes filled his pockets with precious gems from a nearby casket which lay carelessly open, and said: 'This place

13

gives me the willies, Colin. Let's get out before dark!'

Colin laughed and laid aside the vase he had been examining.

'Don't be an ass, Arthur. Why risk our necks in the jungle when there aren't any animals round here?'

'That's just what worries me. Why aren't there any animals here? The place is — is haunted — cursed.'

'You're letting your imagination run away with you.' His companion smiled. 'There are no animals simply because there is nothing here for animals to have an interest in. The place is deserted and waterless and foodless.'

'Then what do you propose to do?'

'May as well sleep right here where we are. We'll be under a roof, and the door opens and shuts. There isn't anything supernatural here; take my word for it. I'll guarantee you anything we come up against will be easily handled by the rifles or the revolvers. Now, let's get something to eat, and call it a day. Tomorrow we can make a complete tour of the city — or as much as we can manage in one day.'

Birnes allowed himself to be persuaded; and the two men ate a little of their dried food, and drank the remains of their water.

Colin said: 'Tomorrow we'll have to make a search for fresh water somewhere. And you can have a go at shooting some game — we'll have to start finding our own now.'

Birnes nodded, silently and moodily.

He had a great deal on his mind.

The darkness over the city now was intense, and the eeriness doubled. Far away in the jungle the nocturnal howling of strange animals could be heard; but here they only served to intensify the utter lifelessness of everything.

Colin yawned, laid down his haversack for his head, said: 'I'd turn in if I were you, Arthur. We don't need that fire in here. We won't be attacked.'

Birnes shivered and heaped more brushwood onto the fire they had lit.

'I'll hang on a bit,' he said, casually. 'One of us may as well keep an eye open. You never can tell.'

Colin grinned at his nervousness and

turned onto his side. Birnes sat motion-less where he was, waiting, his crafty mind running in wild circles, his fingers toying with the riches in his pocket.

A gentle snore issued from the sleeping Colin; and at last Birnes moved. Softly, he picked up one of the rifles: stealthily, he trod towards the sleeping Colin; and then, savagely, crashed down the butt on the other's head! Nothing stirred or moved; Birnes began to carry out the second part of his plan, which was to drag Colin into the edge of the jungle, leave him there for the wild beasts.

Half an hour later, taking all the sup-plies, compass, maps and his handful of gems, he left the forbidden city of Kosan.

By the time day dawned he was a shivering, fearful wreck of a man. The night had been awful, full of strange and frightful noises — and now, alone, he heard them more clearly.

He almost regretted murdering his part-ner — but the thought of the wealth he would retrieve from that dead, deserted city made him plough onwards determinedly.

The morning found him weak and

weary, both from mental and physical stress. Mentally he was not a strong man; his mind was too apt to dwell upon what might happen, instead of upon what need not happen if he took care. Every rustle of the bushes terrified him. Every stirring of the trees above him made him shy forward in uncontrollable panic.

He'd been mad to take the chance of getting back alone; he couldn't face more nights like this; it wasn't possible.

He thought of the man he had left back there, and his tongue licked round his dry mouth as he remembered, and wondered what carnivorous animals were slavering over his still body at that moment.

Birnes never knew how he finally got back to the nearest semi-civilized village. But he did. And from there on he journeyed by river in a canoe, with four men paddling him back to the world which worshipped money.

And at last the twinges of conscience were allayed.

2

The Troubled Lady

Arthur Birnes tilted the thin-stemmed glass and drained his drink appreciatively. He gazed again round the luxurious London hotel room, and his thoughts shifted momentarily back to the lonely city of Kosan, lost in the middle of the Peruvian jungles — and to the man he had struck down and left there brutally.

He was not troubled by conscience; he was not that kind of a man. Whether his blow had killed, seriously injured, or merely stunned Colin, he did not know. He had been too anxious to make good his flight from that cursed city. But he did know that Colin, without compass, map or weapons, could never get back alive. The savage denizens of the forests would quickly rend him, until his torn and lacerated body was picked clean by the circling vultures.

And now there was a task to perform which Birnes looked forward to with considerable pleasure. It entailed a young, shapely, pretty girl, who should be arriving at any moment. Even as the thought of her crossed his mind, the doorbell buzzed.

Birnes screwed his not-bad-looking features into an expression of pleasure shaded with sympathy. He opened the door and stood back for the girl to enter.

She was just as pretty as her photograph had led him to believe — in fact, if anything, prettier. He made her a strangely stilted bow, and took the hand she offered him.

'Mr. Birnes?' asked the girl, anxiously. 'I am Eva Ferguson. I received a letter from you, telling me you had something to say concerning Colin, about which you wished to see me.'

'I have,' he replied gravely. 'Please sit down, Miss Ferguson.'

Her fingers twisted the clasp of her bag; she sat down nervously on the edge of a chair, and shook her head at his offer of a drink. He said: 'Miss Ferguson, please take this drink. What I have to tell you about Colin is — well, it is liable to be a great shock to you, as it was to me when — when it happened.'

'Happened?' She started forward from her chair, her pretty face twisted with anguish. 'Oh, Mr. Birnes! Has — has anything serious happened to — to Colin?'

He sighed and took a drink himself. He said: 'You look a brave woman, my dear, so I will try to break it as gently as I should. I feel sure you would rather know the worst . . . '

She was stiff now, her eyes staring at his face, her fingers quite still and taut on the clasp of her bag. He came over and patted her shoulder, and she said, mechanically: 'Yes. Yes, please tell me without trying to conceal anything. What — what has happened?'

He took her hand, but she shook aside his grasp impatiently. He said: 'I'm afraid — afraid poor Colin is dead, my dear.'

The faint vestige of life remaining in her face left it. She sat there like some statue carved expressionlessly in marble.

Her face had drained of its colour.

When she spoke her voice no longer held the warm, soft tones. She spoke automatically, in a flat, monotonous, choppy voice.

'How did it happen? Did — did he suffer — much?'

'Do you think you really should know?'

'I must know. I must be certain he really is dead. I can't believe it. Please tell me.'

'He died alone,' explained Birnes, infusing a note of misery into his voice. 'I was too late to help him. You knew he intended to find the lost city of Kosan?'

'Yes; I knew that.'

'Well, I met him in Peru, and he remembered me from our schooldays. I was down on my luck, and he was good enough to ask me along with him on the expedition. He often used to talk to me about you: about how, after this adventure, he meant to settle down and marry you. He showed me the photograph he always carried, and I didn't blame him. The only thing I couldn't understand was why, with a girl like yourself at home, he would go wandering round the world on outlandish quests.

'Anyway, we found the lost city of Kosan. It was while I was searching the temple ruins one evening that it happened. He wandered off, unnoticed by me, into the portion of the city which lay in the edges of the jungle. He was foolish enough to go without weapons, and the first thing I knew was the sound of horrible roars and growls, and his voice calling for help from a patch of jungle about two hundred yards away.

'I raced there as quickly as I could, of course; but when I arrived I found only a bloodstained scrap of khaki. I searched until darkness fell, and found no trace of him.'

'He'd been — been — ' stammered the girl.

'Carried away by some wild beast,' supplied Birnes, trying hard to put a quiver into his tone. 'I admit I almost went mad — I actually wept out there in that lost city. But when I recovered I decided it would be of no use to stay there — I came home, and my first thought was to acquaint you with the unhappy facts. I know what a shock this has been to you, and I sympathize deeply.'

'You're — you're sure he's . . . dead?'

'I'm afraid so, my dear. At times I feel almost guilty myself; if only I had known he was going to wander away like that . . . '

The girl struggled to keep calm, fought hard to keep the tears from her eyes. She said: 'No — no, you mustn't blame yourself, Mr. Birnes. Colin was always absentminded when he stumbled on to anything like this lost city. You couldn't have done anything. It was just — just hard luck.'

'I'm sorry I couldn't have broken it more gently.'

'I prefer it this way. It's hard, but I know Colin wouldn't want me to ruin my life over it. He always did say to me: 'Try to forget me, Eva. I'm not worth any woman's love.' That's — that's the kind of — of man he was, Mr. Birnes. He didn't realize that I couldn't forget him, no matter how hard I tried. I'd — I'd have waited until I was old and grey if I'd thought he'd come back to me eventually. But now — '

Birnes adopted a paternal expression and patted her gently on the shoulder. 'I know, my dear. He was a fine, upright man. I don't know how I ever managed to get out of that jungle alive without him.' He broke off, then said thoughtfully, 'Look here. I've an idea; perhaps it would soothe you to hear about our trip into the jungle together. Sometimes it helps to talk, doesn't it? Suppose you come along with me and dine, and we can have a good chat about Colin?'

She shook her head.

'You've been very kind to me, Mr. Birnes, and I appreciate your wanting to help me. But — I feel I must be alone tonight. Perhaps, if you'd care to call on me tomorrow night, we could do as you suggest? I have a lot of Colin's things — souvenirs he picked up all over the world — that you might like to see, and talking about him might help to bring him back in a small way.'

Birnes agreed, and the girl rose and gave him her address. He escorted her as far as the door, and she paused there to say goodnight. The hypocritical Birnes murmured: 'Try not to be too upset about him, my dear.'

But once the door had closed on her, a slow smile broke over his face, and he rubbed his hands and chuckled, feeling like the villain of an old-time melodrama. He gloated as he recalled the way the girl's sheer-silk-clad legs had looked, the way her light costume had clung to her young, innocent figure.

If he was not very much mistaken he had made a good start. She was still too upset yet, of course, but in time . . . the man who had been nearest her fiancé at his death! That was an excellent beginning to a beautiful — friendship. He desired her almost as much as he desired the wealth in the lost city. He remembered those jungle nights when Colin had lain with him beside the fire, staring at the photograph of her; remembered how his pulse had leaped, until a mad ambition to possess her had stolen over him. Birnes had kept those thoughts secret from his companion. For Colin loved her, with a purer, more spiritual love; and once, when an almost-coarse remark had left Birnes' lips about her physical attractions, Colin had given him to understand that any more talk like that would mean blows. So Birnes had wisely curbed his tongue.

He poured more liquor and drank it off. Then he searched the phone book for a number, found it, and picked up the telephone.

'Hello? George Horton? Good man, George. I bet you haven't the faintest idea who's at this end?'

'I haven't,' came a perplexed voice. 'Who is?'

Birnes chuckled, said: 'It's me, Arthur Birnes. Remember?'

'Birnes? Birnes? Why, yes, I do.' The voice wasn't very enthusiastic. 'How are you?'

'I'm great. And listen — I'm giving you the first chance to get in on a grand thing. Can you come round?'

'I'm sorry. I'm rather busy.'

'You'll be sorrier if you pass this up.'

There was a pause, then: 'Very well, if it's important. What's your address?'

Birnes gave it to him and hung up. Then he chuckled again and sat back in his chair to wait for Horton.

George Horton had been at college with him, and had met him once or twice since then. His father had passed away some time ago, leaving him in control of a large firm of jewel manufacturers, and George had made money hand over fist with his astute business mind and his not-too-scrupulous methods. That was why Birnes had called him — he needed someone who wouldn't be *too* scrupulous, and Horton exactly fitted the bill.

He arrived some ten minutes later, wearing spotless evening clothes which fitted his sleek, dark personage like a second skin. If anything, he was foppish in appearance. But underneath that, nails had nothing on him. There was a hard, callous streak in George Horton, as many men had found.

He eyed Birnes with evident contempt, and said: 'Long time since we met — thank God. What do you want to discuss?'

Birnes flushed, but took the insult. 'Yes,

it's about five years since I bumped into you at Epsom, isn't it?'

'And put the bite on me, for ten quid,' hinted Horton, 'which I have never had the pleasure of seeing since.'

'Forget your ten quid,' said Birnes. 'This is worth thousands to you if you'll come in with me.'

'What is?' asked Horton, suspiciously 'I'm not going into anything crooked, Birnes. If that's your idea you can wash it out as far as I'm concerned.'

'It isn't crooked,' explained Birnes 'At least, not all that crooked. It's one of those things like dodging paying your income tax or smuggling things through Customs. I'll give it to you straight: Colin Davis — remember him?'

'Yes; he was the same class as us, wasn't he? Nice chap.'

'If you like that kind of strong, clean-living hero stuff, he was,' agreed Birnes. 'Well, he and I discovered a lost city in the wilds of Peru. Only, unfortunately, he got tangled up with the business end of a wild animal, and that left me in sole possession of the map.'

'You don't seem very upset about his death, do you?' said Horton, staring at Birnes keenly.

'Why should I be? I get the entire boodle now, don't I?'

'Are you on the level about this blessed city?'

'Strictly. Name's Kosan, and it was built presumably by a lost tribe of the Incas who left the parent body. The whole place is running alive with gold and gems; there's millions in it. Here, take a look at these . . . '

He forked in his breast pocket and brought out a small leather case. He opened the press stud, tipped the contents out on to the table top. Horton gasped and picked up a handful of the precious stones, took a glass from his pocket, and studied them.

He whistled softly, said: 'By God! Flawless. Do you know how much you'd get on these, man?'

'Haven't the foggiest. I sold one to a dealer in Brazil on my way home, and he gave me five thousand dollars for it.'

'One like these?'

'A little bigger — a ruby, I think it was.'

'Then he swindled you. This little lot in my hand represents a total value of about eighty thousand pounds. I'll give you that much on the spot.'

Birnes shook his head, decisively, said: 'No thanks. If you're willing to give me eighty, I know they're at least worth a hundred and twenty thousand.'

'Then what the devil have you called me here for?' demanded the other man.

'I'll explain; you'll agree that if a thousand times this amount of gems was unloaded on the world markets, it'd knock the bottom clean out of them, wouldn't it? That's where you can help me; help me to go back with an expedition and get those gems. Help me to dodge declaring the find to the Government of Peru, and help me to distribute them so we won't ruin our own game.'

'And what do I get out of that?'

'Twenty percent of all takings. And that'll be plenty, as you can see by these stones here. How about it?'

Horton said: 'A thing like this will take preparation. We can't dash into it. Just where is this sacred city of yours?'

Birnes said: 'Come into the bedroom — I'll give you a glimpse of my map.'

They rose and went through into the bedroom. Birnes took the map from its place of concealment, but was careful not to let Horton study it too closely. He folded it up, slipped it into his pocket, and they returned to the sitting room.

Birnes was saying: 'You see, George, if we can . . . '

He stopped suddenly, exclaimed: 'Good God! The gems — they've vanished!'

3

Voice on the Line

He stood staring hopelessly at the table on which the assortment of rubies, emeralds, diamonds and topazes had been lying. They were no longer there — nor was the leather case which had contained them.

Horton was the first to recover; three strides brought him through the apartment door and into the corridor. It was deserted.

He ran to the lift; it was on the bottom floor according to the indicator; he took the nearby stairs two at a time and rushed along the lower corridor, which was empty and silent. This led him to the main lounge, and here people swarmed in their dozens.

Further search was useless. He returned to Birnes' room, and found him a bundle of nerves'-end annoyance.

'Gone,' Birnes stammered. 'Just like

that — I never thought anyone would sneak in . . . did you find anyone about?'

Horton shook his head. 'No one to whom suspicion pointed directly,' he told the other. 'But why worry? If, as you say, those gems are only a millionth part of what you can lay your hands on, you can afford to lose them, can't you?'

'You don't understand — those gems were to pay for the new expedition to the lost city. I counted on them . . . '

George Horton coughed, and a hard look crept across his already hard features. Birnes went on wildly:

'Now — now I haven't a penny to equip the party with!'

And then he looked at Horton. Horton looked at him. And before Birnes could even speak, Horton said: 'No thanks, Birnes. Count me out.'

'But George, there's a fortune in it. It wouldn't cost a great deal to fit a party out.'

'Wouldn't it? I'll tell you this much, Birnes: I'm not so sure you haven't worked this whole thing. I remember you of old — I find it damned difficult to forget that ten quid you owe me. You always were a crafty devil, and I'm not being stung by any of your clever stunts. No, I'm out, Birnes. Sorry.'

Birnes said: 'All right, damn you. Don't come in with me. Be clever; you'll regret it. I'm not worrying about losing your help; with the plan I have, dozens of men would be glad to step in for a fifty-fifty cut.'

He reached over for the telephone, and Horton watched him undecidedly. He dialled Whitehall 1212, and got through. He said: 'I want to report a theft.'

Horton watched while he gave details. There was a puzzled frown on his face. He wondered if, after all, Birnes had been on the level about the whole thing. Perhaps it wasn't just a confidence trick to prise some of his loose change off him.

Birnes laid the phone aside, having been told a man would be sent over. He looked in surprise at Horton, said:

'Still here?'

'Look here, Birnes; are you on the level about this?' Horton demanded. 'Because if you are, I might consider coming in with you after all. How much do you reckon would be needed?'

Birnes sneered, and grunted, 'You can get the hell out of here, Horton. I thought I needed your help — but I've changed my mind. There're plenty more fish in the sea.'

'There are.' Horton nodded. 'And you're just the chap to hook them. Suppose we stop quibbling and standing on our dignity? How much, Birnes, to equip your expedition?'

Birnes was rattled; he snarled, 'I've told you. You turned the chance down once. I'm not repeating my offer. Perhaps Issenstahler will be interested in the proposition.'

Horton glared. Issenstahler was his biggest rival; if that fat gentleman got his hands on such an amount of gems as Birnes claimed the lost city contained, he'd make his first job the complete ruination of George Horton's company.

But Birnes was obstinate now, with that strong stubbornness which is so noticeable in weak people. No argument would move him. Horton shrugged, said: 'You'll get a lousy deal from Issenstahler, Birnes. Why not talk it over with me again? Forget what I said — it was just that that robbery didn't seem on the level.'

'What makes you think it is now?' sneered Birnes.

'You. I know you too well to think you'd call in the Yard on a job you'd faked yourself. You're too weak for that — too yellow.'

'Thanks,' said Birnes. 'You're going the right way to get me to reopen my offer again, I don't think.'

'Why be hypocritical? I never could be, and I'm not starting in now, whatever the gain. You know you're yellow — I know it too. No sense in concealing it. I don't care about that; my offer still goes.'

'But mine doesn't. I'm not arguing about it any more, either.'

Horton was about to speak again when the phone rang. Birnes took it up with an annoyed exclamation. The voice which came through was thin and clear, with a metallic quality about it. It was devoid of any tone or feeling, and spoke slowly and deliberately.

'Arthur Birnes, you have just been relieved of the gems you stole from the sacred city of Kosan. You will never see them again, nor will the police ever trace them or the person who took them. But this is merely the start, Birnes; there is more — and worse — yet to come. You will learn that it is unwise to purloin treasure from Kosan. And you will pay also, for the blood you shed there!'

The voice clipped abruptly away, leaving Birnes staring at the receiver with a pallid face. Horton, who had caught the gist of the monologue, suddenly laughed harshly.

'That's damned interesting, Birnes. 'The blood you shed there', eh? Now, what could that have meant?'

Birnes said, 'I — I can't understand it. Who — who could know about that?'

'So you *did* shed blood, there, did you?'

'No, no,' said Birnes, pulling himself together. 'There's something damned uncanny in this, George. Who — what could it be?'

Horton grinned maliciously. 'Who knows? Seems to me I've read a lot about these sacred cities, and unpleasant things happening to those who choose to defile them. Perhaps you've been talking to a ghost, Birnes.'

'Don't be a fool,' quavered Birnes, but his hand trembled as he lit a cigarette. He was remembering his wild flight from the city of the dead, remembering his stumbling retreat through the rough jungle paths and perils, and the conscience-haunted nights before he had reached the outposts of civilisation. Ghosts hadn't seemed so far away then; and that voice had brought it all back to him.

'How about my offer?' asked Horton, breaking in on his thoughts.

'I can't talk about it just now. I want to think, George. Call me tomorrow.'

Horton shrugged again and reached for his hat. He paused at the door, said, 'You suggested this thing to me — and bear in mind that if you don't go through with it, with me as your partner, you'll have more than ghosts to deal with!'

'Is that a warning?' muttered Birnes.

'That's a threat! Good night, Birnes.'

The police inspector rolled in five

minutes after Horton's departure, and Birnes told him as much of the story as he thought was good for him, omitting to mention the telephone call. The inspector apparently was not too hopeful, but promised to conduct investigations, and then he left.

Birnes sat twisting his fingers for a long time then. Until he had received that phone call, his filthy trick on Colin back in Kosan had been thrust into his subconscious. Now it was to the fore again; and, already a weakling mentally, Birnes was not cut out to have murder on his mind.

At long last he mastered himself enough to get up and go into his bedroom; he glanced at the opened pillow-slip where he had, until that moment, kept the map hidden. He decided a change was necessary. Frightened he might be, but his fear had not robbed him of his astuteness. Horton had seen him take the map from that hiding place, and he had no more trust for Horton than Horton had for him. He glanced all round, anxiously, finally decided on his shaving kit in the bathroom. He removed his shaving soap from its metal case, screwed up the map to fit, and placed it in the container, afterwards destroying the soap by the simple means of slicing it into thin flakes and washing it down the bath drain.

He was still uneasy when he returned to the sitting room and poured out a Scotch.

The rustling from the door attracted his attention at once; his eyes shifted fascinatedly to the scrap of paper which was being eased beneath the woodwork into his room. He wanted to rush over and grab it, throw open the door, but his legs stayed fixed to the spot he was in, refusing to obey his brain. He watched for a period which seemed like eternity, until the paper was completely in the room, until the rustling had stopped, and soft footfalls were pattering away down the passage.

Then he moved; picked up the paper; read it.

This is to tell you that you are still being watched. The time is not yet ripe, but it will surely come. There are many different ways: the bite of a deadly insect, a poisoned needle, a knife in the dark hours, a stifling, strangling noose, or . . . but you will find out.

Birnes stared for minutes at that strange communication. It was melodramatic in the extreme — but it didn't seem melodramatic to the man whose life was in the balance. To him it seemed horribly, dreadfully real. A dry sob tore from his throat; he whined. 'God! What — what is it?'

Gathering his frayed courage together he crossed uneasily to the door, threw it open, half-expecting to behold some grotesque form of retribution out there — and gasped at what he did see.

The young lady was tall and graceful, with a cool, sophisticated brand of charm which at any other time would have had Birnes drooling at the mouth. Her eyes were blue and clear, features deliciously shaped, lips red and full over small white teeth. Her furs hung from an expensive costume, and her ridiculous hat shouted out the fact that it was an exclusive.

She had been about to knock, and was as surprised to see the white-faced Birnes as he was to see her.

'Mr. Birnes?'

'I — I'm Birnes. Did — did you push something under my door?'

She looked blank, but said, 'Why, no; certainly not. I was about to call on you. I hoped I'd catch you at home. It's rather important.'

'Did you see anyone — anyone going down the passage away from this door when you came here?' She shook her head. 'I'm rather busy just now, Miss . . . '

'My name is Davis — Inez Davis.'

Birnes started: 'Why, you're Colin Davis' sister, aren't you? He mentioned you often to me.'

'That's why I've come. I don't want to trouble you, but I'm very uneasy in my mind. About — about what happened to Colin in Kosan.'

Birnes went a shade paler. 'Won't you come in?'

He made her comfortable with a drink and cigarette on the settee. 'You know about poor Colin? I intended to write to you tomorrow.'

'Yes, I know. Eva called on me tonight, not long ago, and told me everything. She said she'd seen you, and you'd explained about Colin. But somehow I can't think he really is dead — Mr. Birnes, you didn't actually see him mauled by a wild beast, did you?'

'Not actually. But the bloodstained piece of shirt; the awful snarls and cries for help; and, when I got to the spot, nothing.'

'I still can't think he's dead. We were very close together, Mr. Birnes, and that may account for what I have to tell you. You see, for the last three months I have been having dreams every night.'

'Dreams?'

'More nightmares than dreams — terrible dreams. It all began about the time yourself and Colin must have been near the lost city. I seem to see — in my dreams — a high, gloomy building, filled with old bones in grotesque positions. Then the scene shifts to the interior of what is obviously a house or building of some type unknown to modern civilisation. You and Colin are there; every time I dream my dream you are both there. Colin is lying down, head on his haversack, and you are sitting over a small fire — your face always seems worried about something. Then you get up, pick up your rifle, and walk across towards Colin . . . '

'Yes?' Birnes was leaning forward, hands tense and clammy, sweat clinging in globules to his temples. 'Yes? What then? What happens?'

The girl shook her head slowly. 'I don't know, Mr. Birnes. The dream always stops short there and goes to something else.'

Birnes sat back limply, said shakily, 'What else, Miss Davis?'

She knitted her brows and tried to remember. 'It's all so vague; the first part of the dream is awfully real and lifelike — but the second part hasn't any element of reality in it. I'm surrounded by a white, steaming mist; I can hear weird jungle noises all about me, but I can see nothing but the white mist, shifting and swirling.

44

'Then there is a voice in the mist: Colin's! It seems ever so far away, and it's calling something — something which sounds like '*Inez — Inez —* '. I feel that he's trying to tell me something, and I struggle upwards into the mist, and start walking forward. I can hear his voice plainer then, can actually feel him near me. Then I see his face through the whiteness — and — ' She stopped and shuddered.

'Go on,' said Birnes, hoarsely.

'I always scream then; his face is — is bathed in blood, and his head is horribly smashed in. I — I try hard to hold on to the dream, but I scream every time — I wake up screaming.'

Birnes mopped his brow, said, 'There's nothing unusual in that. I can't see why you should imagine Colin is alive. Clearly your dream is simply inspired by his death and the tragic circumstances.'

'No, it can't be. I dreamed that dream long before I had any idea anything had happened to him. Long before I knew he had really found Kosan — Mr. Birnes, if Colin is dead, he is trying to tell me something! Something important!'

4

Midnight Mission

'I find that hard to credit, Miss Davis,' laughed Birnes, but his laughter was shaky and unnatural, and his eyes were narrowed, furtive, ridden with fear.

The girl held her head in one gloved hand; her voice trembled even as she spoke. 'Of course you do. You didn't know how close to one another Colin and I were. There was never any of the usual brother-and-sister quarrelling between us. But the dreams, Mr. Birnes. How do you account for them?'

He shook his head. 'I won't attempt to; I believe they're part of your unstrung condition as a result of your brother's sad death.'

'You're forgetting the point, though; you're forgetting that the dreams started long *before* I knew my brother was in any danger of dying.'

Birnes was getting rattled and impatient. 'But why come to me? How can I help you?'

'I wondered if perhaps you could tell me whether the places I see in the dream are actual parts of the dead city where Colin lost his life.'

'Really Miss Davis, hadn't you better try to dismiss the matter from your mind altogether? You're only upsetting yourself for no useful reason.'

'No, Mr. Birnes, I can't. I've tried. It just won't work, you see. I feel sure that if Colin is really dead, he is trying to get back to me, trying to explain about something. If the places I see in my dreams fit in with any of the places you visited in Kosan, then don't you see that makes everything more significant?'

Birnes shook his head slowly, but said, 'If it will set your mind at rest, I'll do what I can to help you. Please describe these — these scenes you see.'

She outlined them faithfully and exactly. By the time she had finished, he was feeling weak at the knees, and had to sit down in a chair to control himself. She might almost have been there herself, so clear was her knowledge of the vast, forgotten temple where he had struck her brother. If ever her dream should complete itself — but of course she could prove nothing. People would simply laugh at her. But he knew he might as well start at once to make her believe her night-time visions were inaccurate.

'I can assure you, Miss Davis, that the descriptions you've given me don't fit Kosan at all. I'd advise you to forget all about it, and try to get a good night's rest. We dream some weird things when our minds are upset, and perhaps you have been worrying about Colin for some time, subconsciously.'

She wasn't convinced, and he thought there was something peculiar in her expression as she gazed at him. He rose awkwardly, said, 'Sorry I can't set your mind more at ease. Now, if you'll excuse me, I have an appointment . . . '

She flushed at his rudeness, rose, and walked to the door which he opened for her. In the corridor she paused and looked him directly in the eyes.

'I have a feeling, Mr. Birnes, that that dream of mine *is* important. I feel that sooner or later, I will dream it to the end — I will know what Colin is trying so desperately to tell me. When I do, if you have no objections, I would like to slip round and tell you how it ended.'

'By all means — if I'm still in town,' agreed Birnes. 'But I may not be, you know. I plan to go back to Kosan with an expedition before long.'

'I think I will be in time; and I feel sure you'd like to know how it ends — after all . . . you *were* the last one to see poor Colin alive!'

Was there something in her tone? Something accusing? Rattled, Birnes' nerves leaped with panic; with the alacrity customary to the guilty trying to appear innocent, he snapped: 'What exactly do you mean by that?'

She looked at him in surprise — or was it surmise? He was unable to read her features correctly. 'By what, Mr. Birnes? Have I said something which has annoyed you?'

'No, no,' stuttered Birnes. 'Forgive me.

My own nerves are unstrung as well as yours. Losing Colin was a great shock to me.'

'It must have been,' she told him speculatively. 'But the fact that you are the only one who knows the trail to Kosan will make up for that slightly, won't it, Mr. Birnes?'

Then, before he could control himself sufficiently to answer, she was sweeping away down the corridor towards the lift, high heels clicking on the woodwork, sheer silk stockings straight and wrinkleless over the firm smoothness of her slim legs.

Birnes turned back into his rooms, muttering an oath. As he dressed to visit a night spot, he was wondering if she suspected anything and had guessed he had something to do with Colin's non-return. Perhaps Colin had written to her, mentioning some of Birnes' avaricious traits; perhaps that was what had made her level those accusative hints at him. Or had she merely been talking? Had she been sincere in all she had said, confiding in him without meaning any innuendos? He doubted it strongly.

He threw off his terrors; tonight he meant to have a good time with the remains of the money from the ruby he had already sold. There was still a handsome sum left from that sale; tomorrow he would see about getting hold of Issenstahler and propositioning him. He left his rooms, switching off the lights after him and locking the doors.

★   ★   ★

George Horton turned into a narrow entry off Limehouse and walked casually into a small pub, patronized by peculiar types. There were sailors, crooks, cheap ladies, unorthodox gentlemen, and various others whose backgrounds would have made interesting disclosures. Horton had been there before; it was there that he generally received — from one or two select crooks — quantities of stolen jewellery at low prices.

But tonight he was not out for that; tonight he was anxious to contact a couple of willing lads who wanted to pick up fifty quid for practically nothing. And his luck was in, for over in one corner he found Jerky Konners and Larry Higgins. Looked on as crooked types, they weren't up to much; they didn't lack criminal minds, but they did lack guts. Very much so.

Fortunately, Horton wasn't looking for guts; the job he had in mind was simple, calling for nothing more than a knowledge of breaking and entering and theft. He sat beside them, said, 'What's it to be, boys?'

Jerky — so nicknamed because of his peculiar habit of jumping nervously at any unexpected sound — now rose several inches from his seat, spilling his pint over his knees.

'Cor lumme,' he spluttered, whizzing round, and noting with relief who had accosted him. 'I t'ought it was a nark!'

Horton smiled. 'Why, you expecting to be taken in?'

'Yer never can tell,' said Jerky feelingly. 'Can yer, Higgs?'

Larry Higgins agreed you never could. They ordered whiskies, now the paying was to be done by someone else, and settled back with them. Higgins said: 'If you're looking for stuff, Mr. Horton, I'm sorry, we haven't been doing so well lately. Bust one place last night and only glued onto two quid and a set of stainless knives and forks. Wasn't nothing else small enough to carry worth taking.'

'I'm not looking for stuff, Larry,' Horton told him. 'I'm looking for a couple of likely lads to do a little job for me. There's fifty quid behind it for the lucky parties.'

'Fifty quid? What's the job, Mr. Horton?'

'It's simple. I've brought along a set of skeleton keys with me. One of them is sure to fit the door of the room I want searching. The man who occupies the room has gone out — I watched him go myself, and he won't be back for a time; if he does get back early, I'll be waiting outside the hotel to keep him busy while you come down.'

'You — you want us to break into an hotel room?' stammered Higgins. 'Hell, ain't that risky, Skipper? Some of them hotels have special coppers . . . '

'Not this one, it doesn't. I took the trouble of casing the set-up for you. You can get in the back entrance and come up by the servants' stairs there. It's a third-floor room, number twenty-six. Let yourselves in and start going through anything that might conceal a map.'

'A map?'

'I said a map. I've had a glimpse of it — drawn on thin white paper, and a single word in the top-left corner: PERU. Last time I saw it, it had been hidden in the pillow-slip of the bed, but I don't think you'd find it there now. Get that, and there's fifty pounds in it for you.'

'Each?' questioned Higgins, keenly. 'Or between us?'

Horton smiled, said:, 'Get it and I'll toss you fifty each. Okay?'

Higgins looked at Jerky; Jerky jumped assent; Higgins said, 'Okay, Mr. Horton. Now give us fuller details and we'll get on the job.'

★   ★   ★

'Quiet!' hissed Higgins sharply as they sneaked into the hotel by the rear entrance. Jerky jerked to a standstill and peered at the flight of stairs to the right.

'Is these them?' he said, with a fine disregard for grammatical accuracy.

'They is,' agreed Higgins, with a disregard as fine if not finer.

'Then what are we waiting for? Let's get on with the job.'

Higgins grunted and made sure the coast was clear; then, with him in the lead, they began to take the stairs two at a time, whizzing past first and second floors, until they hit the third landing. It was deserted and silent, and Higgins rubbed his hands, chuckling. The job was as good as done if things were all this easy.

Twenty-six was conveniently handy to the head of the stairs. They crept along, ready to appear nonchalant if anyone stopped them. In the event of that unhappy situation coming to pass, they had their excuse all cut and almost dried. They were plumbers from Cheapside, come to fix a faulty water faucet. To bear this out, Higgins carried a small black bag, which actually contained the tools of his trade.

They gained the door without excitement, and Higgins groped for his skeleton keys while Jerky tried the doorknob experimentally.

'Hey,' he whispered hoarsely. 'It's open.'

It was; Higgins looked surprised. 'Thought Horton said it'd be locked? Must have been mistaken. Let's get inside, quick.'

They were speedy, if cautious; the rooms were in pitch darkness, and Higgins shut the door behind them and produced a pencil torch. He switched it on, swivelled the beam round, and indicated the door to the left. 'You take that door. I'll take the right-hand one. If you draw the bedroom, try the pillow-slips first. All right, get to it.'

Jerky wasn't enthusiastic. He moaned, 'But listen, Higgins, yer know I don't like working alone. I gets nervous.'

'There's nothing to be frightened of,' snarled Higgins. 'Get going like I told you.'

Jerky shuddered and brought out his

own torch. While Higgins entered the bathroom, he crossed to the other door, finding that it led into the bedroom. His torch ray picked out the white linen, and forgetting his nervousness momentarily, he hurried over to the bed, started pulling the pillow-cases from the pillows. There was no map there.

He turned his attention to the dressing table; one after the other he swept out the three drawers, spilling collars and ties and clean shirts haphazardly onto the floor. He was unlucky here too. The questing beam of his torch wandered round the room, past the curtains.

Past the curtains, and stopped! And suddenly came shakily back to rest on the heavy red plush over the windows.

Had that plush moved?

No, it couldn't have. Nevertheless, he started and gave a gasp of alarm. Plucking up his nerve, he quavered: 'Y-you in th-th-there, c-c-come out.'

Nothing stirred except his own heart, which was leaping frantically up and down beneath his soiled shirt-front. He moved half-heartedly over to the window, reaching out his hand to draw aside the curtains and set his mind at ease by revealing the fact that there was absolutely nothing behind them.

Then things happened. He hardly knew what at first; he only knew something smashed against his torch hand, sending the torch skating across the floor, a skittering shred of light in the darkness; something else clasped him lovingly round the neck, and pressure was exerted. His flying feet kicked over a chair, his flying fists pumped futilely at mid-air.

The grip on his throat tightened; then a rock-hard piston shot out of nowhere and cannoned forcibly against his right ear, and he went shooting across the floor after the torch. He started to get jerkily to his feet, felt hands fumbling over his person, opened his mouth to yell, and received a present of the same piston-like fist in his mouth. He hit a door which opened under his weight; then he was out into the living room, sprawling on the floor.

Higgins was just leaving the bathroom, having drawn a blank. He gave his fallen comrade a blank stare, rasped: 'What the *hell* are you doing down *there*? This is no time to play silly games.'

Jerky staggered blindly to his feet; he gasped: 'In *there*. There must be 'alf a ruddy dozen of 'em. Let's get out of 'ere quick. We didn't 'oughter took the job on at all. Me nerves'll be all ter pieces after this.'

And in a panic he rushed for the door, flung it open, and vanished into the corridor. Higgins paused a second longer; but as the door to the bedroom started to open slowly, he gave a loud gulp and followed his heroic comrade. The door shut behind them, and the person in the bedroom suddenly burst into a prolonged rumble of subdued mirth.

Taken as criminals, Higgins and Jerky struck him as being rather funny!

5

The Voice and the Shadow

'Hold on, Arthur. Just a second.'

Arthur Birnes, returning home early from his night-clubbing owing to his worried frame of mind, paused as the call came from the shadows on his right, outside his hotel. The voice was followed from the shadows by a tall figure in evening dress; George Horton came across with a cordial smile and slapped Birnes heartily on the back.

Birnes didn't react favourably. His lower lip twisted into a scowl, and he growled, 'What the hell do you want?'

'I want to discuss that little matter of Kosan,' began Horton.

'You're too late. I've finished discussing anything with you, you damned insulting fool. Get out of my way.'

Horton eyed him speculatively. 'Funny thing what that voice on the telephone said, wasn't it? The blood you shed in Kosan. What could that have meant?'

'It didn't mean anything. Some practical joker who knew I'd been there, most likely.'

Horton nodded. 'I don't want to quarrel, Birnes. I've been thinking over our previous talk, and I've decided I'd like to foot the bill for this expedition.'

'Pity you didn't decide that earlier, isn't it?'

'Yes, it is. I admit it. But it's never too late to mend — or so I am reliably informed by a gilt-framed motto which hangs in my Aunt Agatha's front sitting room, and I'm sure Auntie wouldn't hang up anything which wasn't reliable. Certainly she'd never hang it next to the portrait of her late husband, unless it was essentially honest.'

Birnes sneered. 'Have you stopped me to be *funny*?'

'No, not at all. I'm serious about it. To make up for my earlier derision I'm willing to equip your expedition, come along with you, and make you an immediate and substantial advance on things to come. How does that strike you?'

It struck Birnes as being very liberal; he had had grave doubts as to whether he would be able to persuade the shrewd Issenstahler to invest any money in his scheme. This magnanimous offer from Horton caused him to revise his opinions of that gentleman.

'Well, I might be tempted. Come up to my rooms and we'll — '

'Let's chat here. I feel the need of a spot of fresh air; suppose we have a stroll round the block and see what arrangements we can come to?'

'I'm not doing any strolling,' Birnes told him. 'My feet are killing me. However, if you insist on talking here, go ahead. What percentage of the profits would you expect, and how much advance would you make me?'

Horton appeared to consider, then said, 'Say thirty percent of the profits, and I'd advance you five hundred quid now.'

'Make it twenty-five percent and a thousand, and we'll fix it up at that,' edged Birnes.

Horton smiled peculiarly to himself, and Birnes frowned as he detected that smile. But the jeweller said: 'All right, Arthur. You drive one of those hard bargains we hear so much about — and you don't steer too straight, either — but I'll take a chance on you.'

'Much more talk like that,' said Birnes, satisfied now he had made a deal which suited him, 'and you'll have me squashing the whole thing again.' Horton offered him a cigarette, which he refused. 'Now, I'll have to be pushing on. I'm tired, George. Slip round and see me tomorrow about details — and bring along the money, will you?'

Horton started to detain him with some question, then his eyes caught a glimpse of two unkempt specimens slinking hurriedly out of the entry which led to the rear door of the hotel, and he changed his mind.

'On second thoughts, I won't bother with that deal.'

'What?' stammered Birnes.

'I won't carry it through as planned. I never did trust you, and I can't say you've improved with time. Good night, Birnes.'

'But — but — look here, you can't do this. We have a gentleman's agreement!'

'How can we have,' asked Horton, blandly, 'when neither one of us is a gentleman?'

And, leaving Birnes to gape after him, he hurried after the two crooks.

He caught them up, as arranged, round the next comer, and without speaking the three hurried along until they came to a fairly crowded thoroughfare. Here they drew to the side of the road, and Horton asked eagerly: 'Good work — where is it?'

'We didn't get it,' Higgins told him.

'You what?' gasped Horton, unbelievingly. 'Are you mad?'

'No, we ain't,' put in Jerky, surlily, eyes twitching. 'We didn't get nowheres near it as far as we knows. Why should we 'ave?'

'But, you idiots, I took it for granted you'd got it. You came out so quickly — you couldn't have spent more than a few minutes on the search. Why did you stop?'

Jerky growled: 'You told us it'd be ruddy well safe, didn't yer? Well it wasn't;

64

look 'ere!' He turned sideways to the streetlamp, and Horton saw the blood on his jaw and lips where a hard fist had connected with his face. Jerky went on: 'I'm a bag of damned nerves, that's what I am now. Some cove was lurking in there waiting for us. 'E set about me and give me this 'ere.'

'Some cove? Who? What did he look like?'

'We didn't see him. First thing I knows I was on me back, see.'

'You didn't see him? Yet you claim he attacked you?'

'It was in the dark. First thing I knows I don't know nuffin' except there's a fist as big as an 'ouse 'itting 'ell out of me. Ruddy insult and battery, that's what it was. You an' yer safe jobs!'

Horton cursed for some seconds. He had squashed the last chance he'd had of getting Birnes to cut him in on the deal by erroneously thinking his thugs had done their work well and in record time. Now it turned out he was no nearer getting the map than he had ever been. But he was resilient; he said, 'That's too bad. But we'll try again, boys. I don't know who this chap could have been who hit you, but apparently he wasn't there on any social call himself if, as you say, he attacked you in the dark. Now, tomorrow night we'll take more care.'

'There won't be no tomorrow night for us,' put in Higgins. 'I'm not the man to stand aside when there's fifty quid to be picked up, but it'd cost me that to get my teeth replaced if I got treated like Jerky here. Lucky enough that Jerky's teeth weren't anything to write home about anyway.'

'You don't mean you'd throw away the chance of an easy fifty like that, do you?' exploded Horton. 'Damn it, there's men'll *commit murder* for fifty!'

'You find 'em,' said Jerky. 'And good luck to yer.'

'You pair of weak-kneed rats,' scowled Horton. 'No wonder you never get beyond petty larceny. All right, I'll make it a hundred each.'

'Not for a thousand,' grunted Higgins. 'Come on, Jerky. Let's go.'

And they went, leaving a fuming

Horton trying to think up suitable curses to heap on their rapidly departing heads.

*   *   *

Birnes knew something was seriously wrong the moment he found his room door open; for a second, he was tempted to go and secure assistance before entering, but he thought finally that if someone had been in his rooms, they must surely have left by now. He inserted his hand first of all and switched the light on.

The sitting room appeared not to have been disturbed, except for one overturned chair by the bedroom door. His eyes fell on the door of the bathroom which Higgins had left ajar; sudden panic clutching at his heart, he rushed across to it and inside. His feverish fingers tore open his shaving case, extracted the soap container. He heaved a sigh of relief when he discovered the map intact within. At least they'd found nothing.

He deliberated on whether or not to call the police again, then decided against it for the time being. His conscience was troubled enough without having flat-footed inspectors galloping all over the rooms. He wanted to get into bed and sleep the sleep of the unbelievably unjust, and leave his problems until the more rational light of day could help him to clear them from his mind. He locked his door again, and jammed the handle of a chair beneath the knob. Now, at least, he was safe from further molestation that night.

His mind, as he undressed and donned a peculiarly repellent pair of pyjamas, was busy circling aimlessly about the events of that day. Try as he would, he could not dismiss the matter of that telephone call, that message thrust beneath the door, the vanishing gems, and finally this night search of his apartments. He was still far from arriving at any conclusions when he crawled between the sheets and heaved a gratified sigh.

Bed! What wonders of luxurious softness there were in the reality of that word. How different to those nights he had pitched his invisible tent on some forked tree branch in the Peruvian jungles, and had even then slept with one eye half-open on the lookout for deadly reptiles and similarly threatening forms of wildlife. How different, too, to the stuffy, perspiring, flea-traps of the hotels along the coast, which he had stayed at while awaiting transportation back to America and England.

And with the wealth he would obtain from Kosan, he could laze in indolent luxury for the rest of his natural life. He drove that thought from his mind at once, for he had always been afraid of having to die sometime, and the idea of it unsettled him. In fact, definitely terrified him. The knowledge that, even with all his soon-to-be-gained wealth, he would be unable to avert that death by as much as a day, caused him almost to sweat with fear. He was that much of a coward. The type of man who, in a paroxysm of terror, punches the dentist's nose.

He stiffened suddenly; he had switched off the light at the door; there was no switch above his bed. Now he could have sworn he had heard a movement from somewhere. He lay quite still, breath held painfully, listening.

The sound — one which could have been made by the rustling of the window curtains — was not repeated. He relaxed, almost laughing with relief, allowed his thoughts to wander off again.

Yes, he would be able to buy and sell people like Horton soon. And the girl — Eva Ferguson. What a dish. That was for him, all right. She'd play, with a little of the right kind of persuasion: a few drinks, perhaps; some tearful reminiscing about poor old Colin; and one or two of those little tablets he had obtained from a Peruvian Indian, slipped into her drink.

She wouldn't even know what day it was — or night. But he'd be able to tell her. And when she did come round he could tell her she'd fainted, and then play the same trick again once or twice. His thoughts ran along these lines, and he lay back and gave himself over to his imagination entirely.

He was still thinking that way when, snapping into his dulled consciousness like a high-velocity bullet, came a voice!

It was a hard, toneless voice; a voice similar to the one he had heard over the telephone. It seemed slightly muffled, as if by distance, but the words were clearly distinguishable.

'Why not *now*, Birnes?' it said, seeming to ease out of the darkness from every direction, and clogging the atmosphere with dread. 'Why should you not atone *now* for the blood you spread in your desecration of Kosan?'

A faint yowl of horror trickled from Birnes' throat; he could stir neither hand nor leg to reach the light. He could only lie taut and motionless, straining his bleary eyes about him, fearfully.

There was a soft rustling movement, seeming to come from the direction of the curtains. A darker shadow showed against the darkness of the room. It glided noiselessly towards his bed, stood above him. It was not so much that he could see it, as sense it; it was there, menacing, vengeful.

He forced his dry lips to croak: 'What do you want?'

The shadow made no answer to that

question. Two hands materialized from the gloom; two sets of five fingers crept about his clammy throat. The grip contracted, squeezing his windpipe, making him fight to draw in air.

'You needn't worry,' said the shadow, monotonously. 'It won't be *this way* — and it won't be yet.'

But his hands didn't slacken their grip; they went tighter until Birnes gagged, started wriggling, tried to claw away the arms above him. He could feel himself growing weaker; he could not draw a breath at all now; the fact that the voice had told him it would not be yet, made no difference. The shadow was going on strangling him, slowly and surely.

Suddenly the pressure ceased altogether. The hands drew away. And with a soft patter of footsteps the shadow was gone; Birnes lay limply where he had been left, taking in gulps of air: harsh, searing gulps. His entire body trembled wildly from head to toe; his hands clenched and unclenched spasmodically by his sides. Even Jerky could have done no better.

In the sitting room he heard the sound

of the chair being thrown from beneath the door handle, the sound of the key turning in the lock, and the door closing again.

The shadow was gone; but Birnes knew he would come back; he had heard the quality in the voice, and he was afraid of that quality.

There was no sleep for Birnes that night! Morning found him sitting by the window, drinking recklessly, pale and haggard.

6

Enter Miss Sondgard

Birnes was far too shaken by the preceding events to keep his engagement with Eva Ferguson that evening. He could no more have played hypocrite about her fiancé than he could have said who the strangling hands belonged to.

No, he needed relaxation.

And he had a fairly good idea of where he might do that. He dressed with more care than usual that evening. When he left his rooms he was resplendent in evening dress.

There was a new musical show, first-nighting it at the *Galaxy* theatre. It was, according to the adverts, one of those shows with plenty of spice.

It boasted a cast of fifty, twenty-five of whom were gorgeous gals with gorgeous figures. It was, in fact, exactly the type of thing Birnes felt *would* relax him.

He took a ticket at the box office, tipping the cashier for a return which had come in. Then he wandered into the theatre.

George Horton was the first man he saw!

Horton, by one of those unfortunate coincidences, chanced to have a seat in the same box. And right away Birnes saw it wasn't going to be very pleasant in there as the night wore on.

Horton said, 'Good God, since when have they been letting the riff-raff in this place? I thought it was exclusive!'

Birnes scowled, affecting not to hear the remark. But he noticed the smiles on the faces of the two women who were with Horton, and he boiled with rage.

They were pretty women, pretty in a cheap sort of way. They both wore fur coats — or, at least, both had fur coats hung across the backs of their chairs — and both were well-dressed, the style of their gowns being something which had been thought up by a designer with an eye to brevity about the upper portion of the body. One was about twenty-three, dark-eyed, dark-haired, faintly perfumed, and to a certain extent quiet. Her companion was older, cheaper, and noisier; but, Birnes thought, a woman after his own heart.

By 'after his own heart', he meant that she looked the type who wasn't too particular about her morals. And Birnes liked women who weren't too particular about their morals; he wasn't burdened in that way himself.

There was a few minutes to go before curtain time; Horton spent them by holding a discourse with his women. He was already convinced that Birnes had somehow disposed of his partner in the hidden city, and that conviction grew the more he thought things over. He watched Birnes' face while he spoke.

'Have you ever heard the old adage,' he said, 'about dead men telling no tales?'

The dark-haired girl looked at him curiously. She said, 'What brought that up, darling?'

'I was thinking of a friend of mine — no, not a friend. He isn't what you'd term a 'nice' person. I wondered if he believed in that saying.'

The girl laughed, said, 'What if he did?'

'That's the point,' replied Horton, slowly. 'If he did believe in it, perhaps he might have put it into operation!'

'You — you mean — murdered someone?'

The dark girl was horrified. Horton nodded. 'That's about it. This man I spoke of — he isn't a very scrupulous chap.'

'Are you?' grinned the cheaper girl.

'No, I don't suppose so, in a way. But murder's a bit beyond the pale, don't you think?'

'I don't know — I often wanted to murder a man I once knew. I was rather fond of him, and just because he happened to find a man in my room, he refused to have anything more to do with me. It didn't matter how I pleaded; he put on one of those virtuous acts. You know: strong, silent, hero, deeply grieved by wicked, designing woman.'

Horton had been watching Birnes closely, and at his first remark had been gratified to see the other stiffen, tense;

then, when the curvaceous girl had started to air her views, Birnes had relaxed once more.

He had, in fact, more than relaxed. As the girl continued to lay bare her lack of conventionality, Horton saw a gleam of desire light up Birnes' eyes. He turned his head away: a scheme was hatching in his mind!

The first half started, and for a time the occupants of the box lost themselves in the show. It was, as claimed, full of those gorgeous eyefuls, and Birnes, forgetting his fears, drank it all in avidly. It was the first time he'd seen a girly show since leaving for Peru, and he didn't wish to miss a curve or angle of this one.

The first half drew to a close at last, and the lights went up. Horton turned to him. 'Enjoy it, Birnes?'

Birnes didn't answer at once. He distrusted the tone of voice Horton spoke in — it was too friendly by far after his former cracks. 'It was quite good.'

'I'd like you to meet some friends of mine,' said Horton. 'Miss Sondgard, and Miss Bracemain.'

The two girls fluttered their lids at Birnes; the louder of them gave him a wide, blue-eyed stare, with a good deal of admiration in it. Birnes got hot under the collar and acted the gentleman. His animosity toward Horton suddenly vanished.

'How about a tiddley, Birnes?'

'I think I could stand one. Will the ladies join us?'

The ladies, it appeared, would.

But on the way to the bar, while Birnes held forth pompously to the dark girl, Horton drew the other — Miss Sondgard, she of the improperly constructed morals — to one side. He spoke to her in low tones as they followed Birnes and the other girl.

'Listen, Daisy . . . '

She listened.

'That chap . . . '

'Mr. Birnes?'

'Of course Mr. Birnes. Who'd you think I meant? He's got something I want.'

'He hasn't a thing *I* want,' said Daisy, disdainfully.

'Hasn't he? I thought perhaps he had

the way you looked at him . . . '

'You know that's my stock glance.'

'You'll be doing it once too often one of these days,' said Horton.

She grinned. 'What do you mean, *one of these days*?'

Horton brought the conversation back to the subject.

'I fancy you'd like to earn yourself a hundred pounds, wouldn't you?'

She ogled him, not without surprise. 'Oh, Mr. H! What would Dolly say if she heard that? I thought *she* was your big moment, and I was just along because I'm her friend and I haven't anything better to do. Sure, I'd like to earn a hundred — but not the hard way!'

'How do you mean, the hard way?'

'I mean I don't care how I earn it so long as I don't have to work for it. Get me?'

'Yes, I get you. It's easy — all you have to do is work your way in with Birnes.'

'That guy in front? Listen, that's what I call the hard way!'

'You're wrong. Birnes won't be hard to flatter. Flatter him into thinking you're interested in him. He is in you already.'

'Nothing doing. A hundred's a hundred, and nobody knows it better than me, but if you think I'm going to spend the evening with that long-winded amateur gentleman, you're crazy!'

'You don't have to do so. I'll try to get him drunk, then you can easily work on him later.'

'Work on him? You're talking in riddles. What is it you want that he's got? And how're you going to get it by giving him a burnt offering like myself?'

'Well, the idea is for you to get him maudlin . . . Get him to talk to you. Tell him what a great guy he is, and ask him if he's ever travelled. After he's started talking, he'll most likely tell you about Peru and the lost city of Kosan . . . '

'What a glorious evening!'

'You could take it for a hundred, couldn't you? The big idea is to get him to show you the map he has — a map of Kosan, the hidden city of the Incas.'

'Who were they?'

'Oh, some people who used to live long ago.'

'What do I do then, after he's shown me his map?'

'You get it . . . '

'I do?'

'That's the notion. You notice where he stacks it, you coax him to sleep; if you get him drunk, that won't be difficult.'

'I hope you're right.'

'When he's all tuckered out, snoring his head off, you get the map. You bring it to me — I'll give you a hundred pounds for it, on the spot.'

'Make it two.'

'You'll do it?'

'I'll do it. On the understanding you pay for any damages I may get in doing it. But suppose this explorer of yours refuses to get pickled? What then?'

'He'll be soused before he leaves here, then you can finish the job at his place.'

Birnes and the dark girl were already at the bar when they went in. Birnes was chatting to her, but he turned expectantly as they entered. Horton said, 'We met a chap — insisted on talking to us about something or other. Mine's Scotch.'

He nodded to the dark girl, Dolly, and

she obediently moved over towards him. Daisy took the stool she had vacated, and Birnes showed his pleasure.

'I'd rather hoped I'd get a chance to speak to you, Miss . . . Sondgard, isn't it?'

'That's it. I was born — confidentially — Daisy Potts, but I don't think Potts quite good enough for a girl in my profession, do you?'

'Er, what is your profession, Miss Sondgard?'

'Me? I'm a model — artists' model.'

'You like the work?' he asked, wishing he were an artist.

'It's all right. Bit cold, and one often gets cramp. But it isn't really work. I don't like work.'

'I sympathize with you, Miss Sondgard. I myself am a — well, I expect you might call me an adventurer,' he said pompously.

'Oh, how thrilling! What kind?'

'Mainly exploring,' he told her, gratified by her shining eyes. 'I — hem — I think I've been pretty near everywhere.'

'You must be immensely rich,' she said,

'to be able to do that.'

'I get by,' he admitted handsomely. 'I expect to be the richest man in England, if not the world, soon.'

'Mr. Birnes! You *don't* mean that?'

'I do, I do.'

'But — but how?'

He glanced about. 'I can't explain that — but it all hinges round a lost city in Peru.'

'How frightfully interesting — do tell me more.'

He shook his head. She pouted. But she chuckled inwardly. The man was a fool. He couldn't keep it to himself here in public; what wouldn't he let out when she'd got him alone and drunk? She moved closer. '*Do* call me Daisy, Mr. Birnes.'

'I will, if you'll call me Arthur,' he replied, warmly.

Daisy Potts winked into space, and moved closer still . . .

7

Night of Terror

'Curtain's up,' announced Horton. 'Coming?'

Birnes stood up to go, and became aware of Daisy's detaining fingers on his coat sleeve. He paused.

'We don't want to go back *there*,' she murmured. 'We can have ever so much more fun ourselves, can't we?'

Birnes thought it highly probable. 'I think we'll have another drink, Horton, if you haven't any objection to my taking your guest from you for a while.'

'I haven't any,' Horton replied. 'Go ahead.'

He and the dark girl left, and Birnes and Daisy were alone at the bar. She moved nearer than ever, and now she was pressed side by side with him. He cleared his throat and ordered fresh drinks.

Daisy's gin and limes, being almost totally composed of lime-juice, went down one after another without even affecting her. Birnes' double Scotches went down in time with her drinks, and so far he seemed quite unmoved. But now she played her trump card.

'Two large ports, please,' she called to the barmaid. 'And make them really large.'

'Hold on,' said Birnes. 'I can't take port on top of what I've had.'

'Oh, please, do. I want to drink a toast, and I believe all toasts must be drunk in wine to be sincere. Besides, you're kidding me about not being able to take it — a man of your experience couldn't get drunk if he wanted to, now, could he?'

Birnes swelled: he liked to think he could hold his liquor. At the back of his mind was a sneaking feeling that he would regret that port, but he lifted the glass gamely.

'All right, my dear,' he condescended with a leer. 'What's your toast?'

'It's to us,' she told him. 'To us, and the night, and romance!'

He drained the glass negligently, and felt a momentary inward qualm which he effectively concealed. She merely sipped hers, then ordered more gin and lime, and whisky for him.

Reckless now, he went the whole hog; while the show roared on out front, they sat and drank steadily. At last, the barmaid said, 'Sorry, we have to close now. It's ten.'

Birnes blinked a trifle dizzily. He looked at Daisy, and she seemed to be all teeth and smile, and a mile wide. She wavered a bit, giving a distorting effect.

He hoisted himself to his feet, and she grabbed his arm. He said, 'Ten? Is it any use going back to see the rest of the show?'

'No, that would be silly. It finishes in about half an hour or so.'

'Then is this where we part?' he asked, questioningly.

She affected coyness. She simpered, 'Not if you don't want us to part just yet, Arthur dear.'

He didn't feel at all steady, but he persuaded himself it would pass off. He hiccupped suddenly, and she giggled. He said, 'Where do we go from here?' In spite of his dizziness he felt on top of the world, and was prepared to make a night of it.

'Have you anything to drink at your rooms?' she asked.

'I think so — yes, some Scotch — but — '

'Then should we — ought we to go there?'

He patted her affectionately. He said admiringly, 'I like you, my dear. You're so natural.'

'Oh, don't be a silly, Arthur. It hasn't a thing to do with being natural. It's just that I haven't ever met a man like you before. You're so big, and brave, and strong.'

He thought so too, and he was pleased that he had at last met a woman who saw eye to eye with his own views. So far he hadn't come across any other woman who had thought him big, and brave, and strong.

He walked uncertainly to the cloak-room and checked out his coat. He didn't feel quite up to putting it on, owing to the way the place seemed to be undulating about him, so he threw it across his arm and walked out to the foyer.

The doorman had already found them a cab and they piled in; Birnes, not without a little assistance from his companion. He giggled a great deal in the cab, and was slapped jokingly three times.

Daisy giggled back. 'You *are* naughty, Arthur.'

They reached his rooms; getting out of the cab, he fell and measured his length on the pavement. Daisy helped him up and dusted him off, and guided him to the door. As the lift shot upwards he suddenly felt sick. He clutched the girl for support, and she put an arm about him.

They made it along the passage to his door, somehow; he found the key, gave it to her, she fitted it in the lock, and they went inside. She dumped Birnes on the divan, poured whisky from the bottle she found, and sat beside him.

But there was no need to give him the whisky; he was groaning now in the most soulful fashion. His features had gone a perspiring white, and his brow was hot and clammy.

'Sorry,' mumbled Birnes. 'Burrp! Sh-shorry. Lishen — bedder not shtop here — you — bedder go — home — I feel — ulp! — f-f-fever — malaria.'

'Oh, Arthur, I believe you're drunk,' she cried.

'Nun-no, f-fever — abroad — be all right — ugh!'

He suddenly got up and made a dive for the bathroom, and she smiled to herself. When he finally came out he looked white and done for. He sat down heavily beside her.

'F-fever,' he muttered.

'Of course,' she said sympathetically. 'I was only kidding when I said you must be drunk. Suppose you have a nice sleep? You must be tired.'

He shook his head; but added to the words she spoke was the comfortable feeling of his head being pulled down to her ample bosom, the softness against his ear, and her hand caressing his temples. He mumbled, drowsily, 'You're staying?'

'I couldn't leave you here alone with malaria, could I?'

He slumped more on to her, and she

continued to stroke his head. His breathing began to get regular; she remained quite still. At last he was asleep — a deep, worn-out sleep.

Daisy grinned down at him, gently eased herself from under him, and allowed his head to fall softly on to the cushions she had readied. He showed no sign of wakening. She gazed about thoughtfully, and her eyes rested on a thick wooden walking stick by the door. She picked it up, weighed it. This was an unusual job for her, but she was tough enough for it. She found a discarded shirt in the bedroom. She wrapped it round the heavy handle of the stick. She dared not risk him waking while she was searching. Unfortunately he had gone too soon to reveal the hiding place of the map.

She settled him nicely on the divan, then stepped back a pace; she raised the stick and studied him thoughtfully. Where to hit? Somewhere that would make sure — base of the neck? She leaned his head slightly to one side, took a stance like a golfer about to drive. There is little doubt that with the weight behind her arm, Birnes would have had his neck dislocated had that blow landed. But it didn't.

'I beg your pardon . . . '

She spun towards the door, which stood open. In the doorway stood a woman — an attractive woman, but with a sober, serious face.

The noise woke Birnes; partly sober now, he stared at the weapon Daisy held.

'What . . . ?'

'I'm sorry,' stated the woman in the doorway. 'I had no idea you had company.'

Birnes was shaken, and sobered still more by the attitude of Daisy, who stood frozenly where she was, stick still raised.

'Daisy — what — why, you — ' He scowled, suddenly realizing the truth. 'Horton put you up to this — the damned — tell him if he doesn't watch out I'll have the law on him — and get out before I turn you in!'

Daisy dropped the stick, picked up her coat. *Bang!* had gone her two hundred. At the door, she turned and said, 'You stinkin' slob,' in finest East End.

Then she brushed past the woman in the doorway with a nasty snort, and vanished from sight. The woman came right in unceremoniously and took a chair. Birnes snapped, 'Miss Davis . . . what do you want?'

'I called to have a chat with you, Mr. Birnes. To, as it were, report progress.'

'I don't think there's anything we can profitably discuss — I'm far too busy a man to waste time on dreams . . . '

Inez Davis said, 'So I see. But in this case . . . '

'I'm sorry. I can sympathize with you in the loss of your brother, but you aren't doing any good carrying on in this manner. Added to which, I object to you bursting in like this.'

'Perhaps it's as well for you I *did* burst in,' she told him.

'How did you happen to find the woman about to attack me?' he said suddenly, struck by a thought. 'You couldn't have knocked?'

'I didn't knock. As a matter of fact, I saw her through the keyhole,' said Inez calmly.

'Really, Miss Davis!' exploded Birnes. 'Am I to take it you are in the habit of peering through keyholes?'

'In your case, yes.'

'May I ask why?' he grated nastily.

'You may. I don't trust you, Mr. Birnes.'

'You — *what?*' He gasped.

'I don't trust you. I feel quite certain that your story of what happened to my brother is false — '

'How dare you!'

'Because I believe you had a hand in his death. Because of the dream — *the dream*, Mr. Birnes! His spirit is troubled, cannot rest! That is why he tries, tries hard to come back, to tell me, to point his finger of accusation at someone . . . '

'At me?' Birnes sneered.

'At you,' she acknowledged calmly. 'That is what I believe.'

'You aren't by any chance looking for an action for slander to be brought against you, are you?'

'I'm not interested in the steps you take to quell my suspicions.'

Birnes growled angrily. 'Then what are

you trying to do?'

'I came here to say that I've thought your story over again, and I'm less satisfied with it than ever. My brother is trying to get back, Mr. Birnes. He will tell me.'

'Dead men don't tell tales,' sneered Birnes.

'No?' Her eyes regarded him curiously. 'Sometimes dead men tell . . . I know of one or two instances in which men have been haunted . . . '

Birnes rose to his feet; said, 'If you don't mind, Miss Davis, I'm rather tired.'

She gazed at him for almost a minute without moving. Then she got to her feet, and tapped her way to the door. She turned there, looked back. 'Mr. Birnes, that dream will have an ending.'

'Good *night*, Miss Davis.'

She walked out.

Birnes brushed a hand across his brow; he felt hellish. He crossed and locked the door after her, switched off the light, and went into his room. He undressed slowly and climbed into his pyjamas. A sudden fear struck him; he seized the stick Daisy had discarded, pulled the curtains aside,

95

and heaved a sigh of relief when the blank window was revealed.

He got into bed, and didn't dare turn off the bed lamp. He tossed and turned again, his mind running in circles. What the devil was going on? Where did he stand with all this?

Horton, after the map, setting thugs and women on to him. The mysterious strangler. Inez Davis, damn her, with her tales about dreams and suspicions. He groaned and pummelled the pillow into softness again.

Dead men tell no tales!

Or do they?

Dead men tell . . .

Could it be possible that Colin Davis was coming back from beyond the grave, coming back to haunt Birnes, to reveal the whole of his dastardly murder to his sister? There must be something in it all: her dream tallied so exactly with the events leading up to the murder; tallied perfectly, in fact. And what if the dream did finish truthfully? What then, when she went round making wild accusations against him?

Could he risk suing her? No, better laugh it off; ignore it as the raving of a demented woman, deranged by the untimely death of her brother, and somehow entangling his best friend who had been with him last into her insane nightmares.

Almost two hours after he retired, he fell into an uneasy slumber.

And this time he dreamed himself. He was in the jungle again, back amongst squawking, shrieking parakeets, with Davis beside him. Ahead, like a mirage in the clouds, lay the lost city of Kosan! Kosan the golden. Kosan, the fabulous, get-rich-quick termination of their journey.

But a figure appeared in the sky before it, held out a misty hand in a gesture of warning. A woman's figure — Inez Davis.

They stopped, and the figure vanished. And as Davis stared at where it had been, Birnes struck him!

He dragged him into the city, into the square, to the pit down which Kosanites had thrown their dead. But as he leaned forward to watch the other thud to the bottom, his own foot slipped, and with a shrill, echoing scream he plunged down into the foul depths. Down and down he whirled, spinning, twisting, in a timeless flight into nothingness. He alighted on something soft and squirmy.

It was dark, and he lay where he was in a frenzy of terror. There was an unclean grave stench about the place, and the rattle and scrape of dried bones grated on his nerves. He felt the substance beneath him move: slimy, flabby, clammy! Suddenly the place was illumined by a red, awesome glow; his terrified eyes beheld that which was beneath him. A soft, sluggish mass of grey matter, like a pool of some hitherto unknown substance. But protruding from it were heads — oh, God! What heads! Heads with rotting, sightless eyes, with broken, jagged teeth, with thin shreds of decaying flesh stripping from them.

Heads which continually moved and rolled and submerged with the motion of the pool in which he lay. Dead, yet living; blind, yet seeing; skull-like, yet grinning; grinning at him, at the fact that he was there among these loathsome creatures of the subworld. Arms reached up and out: skinny, skeletal arms, reaching to drag him down into it. To claim him as one of them.

Voices, macabre, sepulchral, toneless, welled up in a mad, murmuring chorus of exultation. The stench forced a way into his nostrils, made his eyes water feebly; the hands' crooked, clawing fingers poised to rip and wrench him down into the miasmic stuff of dissolved life and decaying death.

They had him! The fingers hooked into his clothing, into his quivering flesh, and cavernous mouths opened in evil grins. He felt the stuff closing about his chest, felt the clamminess of it about his neck.

A phrase kept running through his mind with terrifying consistency — they were chanting it, horribly, frightfully, in deep, dead voices:

'Down among the dead men, down among the dead men, down among the dead men . . . down . . . down . . . down . . . '

'Oh God, oh God!' babbled Birnes, beating the surface of the nauseous plasma which bubbled and sucked about his chin. Then his head sank swiftly, with a last plopping sound, and unseen hands held him down as the stuff streamed into his throat, crushing back his wild, voiceless screams.

He awoke; screams and shrieks and foul imprecations were still wrenching from his parched lips; his clawing hands were tearing at the flesh of his throat; and an unbearable sense of oppression lay over the room.

He flung off the blanket, lay cold and panting, on the bed. He fought to regain his nerves, fought to drive away that fear,

Something had awakened him; something had dragged him out of his horrible D.T. bout. There it was again — telephone. How long had it been ringing, and who could it be? Who could be calling him in the early hours of the morning?

But the thought of hearing the sound of a human voice again brought him from the bed and over to the phone. He picked it up with weak, trembling fingers.

'Birnes s-speaking . . . '

There was nothing human about the

voice which came over! Thin and inhuman, it was the same voice he had heard over the phone once once before . . .

'Dead men tell, Mr. Birnes,' it intoned monotonously. 'Dead men *tell*. Your time is fast approaching. Your sacrilege, your wanton spilling of blood, all will be avenged. Dead men tell . . . '

The phone clattered from Birnes' hands, and with a nerveless shriek he fell in a complete blackout to the floor.

And from the other end of the line came a soft chuckle!

★   ★   ★

'Oh, Mr. Birnes!'

Birnes turned round, startled, as the voice cut across his ears. He was in the restaurant next to his rooms. The food he had ordered lay untouched before him, and his hands were clenched on the cloth. He had been seated here for some time, and now the effect of the previous night was wearing off a little. But his face was still white and ill-looking. And the girl who had called out to him, and was moving towards his table, gave him a compassionate look.

'Are you all right, Mr. Birnes?' she asked gently. 'You look a little ill.'

Birnes forced a smile, said, 'Hello, Miss Ferguson. Yes, I'm well enough, thank you. I had a rather heavy night, though; working late and all that.'

'I was coming to see you when I chanced to spot you in here,' she explained. 'I waited quite a time for you last night. You didn't come over.'

'No, I'm sorry. As I said, some business came up at the last minute. I should have phoned, really. I meant to, but . . . well, I really am sorry, Miss Ferguson. Forgive me.'

'But of course I will. You're forgiven.' She smiled. 'Have you finished your business now?'

He nodded.

'Then — then would you be free for tonight, say?'

'I think so. Yes, I think I could get along without fail tonight — if you think I'm worth having along after the way I let you down.'

'Oh, please, do come. You know, there's so much I want to ask you about — about — ' She broke off, bit her lip. He patted her hand on the cloth, and she did not withdraw it.

'I understand. I was his best friend, and you his fiancée. We two must try to console each other, mustn't we?'

'That's how I feel. Talking helps.'

'I'm sure it does.'

'And — I'm upset. Inez upsets me. She has some absurd idea that he — he's trying to come back from — from the grave!'

Birnes shuddered in spite of the shaft of sunlight which was playing through the window on them. He said, 'I'm afraid Inez is a little hysterical about all this. Don't you think so?'

She nodded. 'I — I think she — she's letting her grief make her dream things.'

He shook off his momentary tremor.

'Forget Inez. Forget her silly stories. A pretty girl like you are shouldn't allow herself to be influenced by a foolish, fantastic woman like Inez.'

She didn't reply, but seemed to agree

with his words silently. She got up, extracted her hand, and said, 'You'll come tonight then?'

'Count on it. I won't let you down this time.'

She smiled a little, and it was surprising the way it added to her beauty. 'Thank you so much, Mr. Birnes. You're so kind. I can't imagine what I'd do without you to stand by me.'

He watched her walk out, examining the line of her sweet young figure. And beneath the table he rubbed his palms together. Yes, he certainly *wouldn't* let her down tonight . . .

8

The Ghost

Birnes turned up at Eva Ferguson's home that night at about seven-thirty. She was expecting him, and greeted him with a pleasant smile, if a somewhat subdued one.

They took dinner alone together: her father, she explained, was out of town, and her mother had been dead for many years. Only she and the servants were at home, and she had asked them not to disturb her and her visitor after they had dined.

They sat in the drawing room and talked. She was full of Colin, and Birnes pandered to her desire to hear about him, meanwhile subtly — he thought — working in odd remarks to show that he too admired her.

She didn't seem to be offended by his forwardness; and later, when she suggested cocktails, she took a position beside him on the divan, quite naturally. To her it was natural — but it filled Birnes with a raging desire for her, to feel the soft, voluptuous nearness of her figure against him, alone like that.

But he was cautious; he didn't mean to lose Eva that way; he would wait until she consented to dine at his rooms, then he could try . . .

'Yes, Miss Ferguson,' he said, in answer to some question, then stopped and smiled and said, 'It's really rather silly us calling each other by our formal names, isn't it? Do you mind very much if I call you — Eva?'

'Of course not, Mr. Birnes,' she said, blushing slightly.

'And in return you'll have to call me Arthur,' he told her. 'After all's said and done, we had a lot in common — Colin, I mean. We both thought the world of him, and we both feel worse about his death than we care to show openly. I'm sure he'd have wanted us to be good friends.'

'I think he would too.' She nodded. 'That was what I liked most of all about Colin. He wanted to be everyone's friend.

It was so awfully hard for anyone to quarrel with him — he just wouldn't argue.'

'No,' agreed Birnes. 'He had a way of talking one out of things, and it generally worked.'

They chatted on of Colin and his personality. Time flew; and outside it was now dark, except for a lemon-shaped moon which was every so often partly obscured by wispy clouds.

Birnes was facing the curtains; they were not drawn, and he had a view of the long lawn giving on to a high wall at the far end.

That was how he saw the ghost!

And even in those few seconds as it flickered whitely before his eyes out there in the garden, he wondered if he was having hallucinations.

He didn't believe in ghosts; but the idea that he might be becoming mentally deranged — seeing things — worried him almost as much as if a ghost had walked right through him.

He could only see the face plainly, outside the French windows. But he didn't need more than the two seconds it flickered there to be quite certain it was — Colin's face!

Not only his face, white and strained, but his head was scarlet with blood at the front where the rifle butt must have landed on the night Birnes had played his scheming tricks. And his eyes — they were grim, sunken, accusing, staring in at Birnes.

Stunned, Birnes sat gaping, mouth open; and the ghost — if it was a ghost — flitted past the windows and was gone.

A strangled, choking gasp tore from Birnes' lips; his hand flew to his forehead and he half-rose.

'Mr. Birnes? Arthur? Whatever's the matter?' asked Eva, in some alarm at the pallid expression on his face and the glassiness of his eyes. 'You look as if you'd seen a ghost!'

'I have,' said Birnes, hollowly. 'Outside the — the windows — Colin — '

She spun to follow his gaze, but the apparition had gone. She turned back again, said, 'Your nerves are strained. Have another drink, Mr. Birnes.'

He sat down again. 'Thanks. It may have been an hallucination. It did seem real, though. You — you don't believe in anything like that, do you?'

'Not myself. But Colin's sister is a very ardent spiritualist. She's had dreams about Colin, you know.'

'I know. She called to see me.'

'She did?'

'Last night after you'd left. She said you'd told her about our meeting and Colin's death, and she thought the dreams she'd had might have a bearing on it all.'

'But what bearing could it have?'

He shook his head, swallowed the brandy she gave him. His hands fumbled with his cigarette case, and she offered him one of hers. She lit it for him and watched him draw jerkily at it.

'Don't worry,' she said, allowing her hand to rest on his arm soothingly. 'Even if it was a ghost — or, shall we say, a spirit? — we needn't fear it. Colin wouldn't wish his friends any harm, I'm sure of that.'

'No, but — ' Birnes cut his remark short.

'But what?' asked Eva, interested.

'Nothing, nothing. I suppose it is my nerves all on edge. God knows the time I had beating a way back through that jungle. It's no wonder the lost city was never found until we forced our way to it.'

She was about to reply when the door of the drawing room opened and Inez Davis walked in.

'I slipped over to ask you if you'd . . . Oh! Mr. Birnes.'

Birnes stood up. Eva said, 'Mr. Birnes and I were talking about Colin, Inez dear.'

'I hadn't any idea you had — er — company. I can call some other time.'

'No, don't go,' pleaded Eva, rising herself. 'Come in and join us, Inez. There's nothing private about the conversation.'

Inez came in. She didn't seem unduly pleased to see Birnes again; and Birnes, for his part, was annoyed by her intrusion. But he gallantly stood aside and said, 'Sit here, Miss Davis. It's a pleasure to meet you again.'

She glanced at him, a half-smile on her lips. 'Is it really?'

He ignored the inflection in her voice,

found himself an armchair and took that. Eva joined Inez on the divan, curled her legs up beneath her, and said, 'Funny you should happen along like this. We were just talking about you.'

'About me?'

'Mmmm. I was telling Arthur — that is, Mr. Birnes — about your belief in spirits. Not the bottled kind, of course — the ones who flit about churchyards at night. The genuine variety, if they can be called genuine.'

'I'm sure Mr. Birnes must have been very bored. He doesn't look at all the type of man to be interested in things of that nature. What on earth brought such a topic up?'

'It was Colin, really; your dreams . . . You see, Mr. Birnes thought he saw — well, a ghost. It sounds silly, but — '

Inez Davis had tensed in her seat, and was staring at Birnes.

She said, quietly, 'You saw Colin? When? Where?'

Birnes felt uncomfortable; there was something about the girl he didn't like; something behind her look when she gazed at him, which made him feel she knew him for what he really was, and was waiting for her chance to expose him to the world. He mumbled, 'It was just an illusion. I thought I saw him outside the windows, but there may be a possibility that the whole thing was due to my overstrung nerves.'

'No!' Her face was tense and set, staring at the windows now. She said, 'No, you saw him, I feel sure you saw him. I knew it when I came up the driveway — I could feel strong forces at work here. You saw him without doubt, Mr. Birnes. What — what did he look like? Was he transparent, or had he a cloudy quality?'

'I couldn't swear to that,' said Birnes, uneasily. 'I caught the merest glimpse of him, a second or two, no more.'

'Was he — injured in any way? Any marks on him?' Now her voice was so intense that Birnes felt sweat breaking through on his hands.

'He wasn't injured in any way,' he lied. 'Looked a bit pale, but otherwise just as I saw him last.'

Inez Davis walked to the window, threw

it open, looked out. She stood there motionless, head back, eyes closed, for long minutes. Finally she closed the window again and returned to her seat.

'He was there,' she said. 'I can feel atmosphere all round this house. He's trying to reach us, I know it. Something's worrying him, he wants to tell us something — perhaps about what happened to him after he — vanished.'

'That's *ridiculous*,' burst out Birnes, coming to his feet, the palms of his hands perspiring freely against the stem of the glass he held. 'Mumbo-jumbo, Miss Davis. Surely you can't believe in it?'

'I do believe, Mr. Birnes. Firmly. I'm also convinced Colin will get through to us. He's strong, and has an unshakable will. If there is something important to be revealed, be sure he will manage it somehow.'

'How about you, Eva?' Birnes demanded. 'Do — do you believe that too?'

'I don't quite know,' Eva said uncertainly. 'Inez has taken me to several spiritualistic meetings, and I must admit some extraordinary things have happened.'

'Table rapping, spirit photographs,' scoffed Birnes. 'They can all be fixed.'

'I know they can; but other things happened too. Things which couldn't possibly have been fixed — at least, I don't think they could.'

Birnes sneered openly. He said, unpleasantly, 'Huh! I can quite understand people practising charlatanry for money, when they have to make a living somehow. But I can't for the life of me understand a well-to-do and intelligent woman such as yourself, Miss Davis, going in for that kind of tommyrot. Not in any circumstances.'

Inez Davis had risen to her feet, her face compressed. Eva said, 'Oh, Mr. Birnes. That's rather rude of you.'

Birnes realized he had allowed his temper to run away with him. 'I'm sorry. I apologise. It's simply that I can't credit that sort of thing myself.'

'But didn't you tell me that when you reached Kosan you felt strange influences yourself?' said Eva accusingly.

'Yes, but that was due to the surroundings and our frame of mind, I think. Certainly not to any spirits — however, I should really make allowances for other people's beliefs, I know. I apologise again, Miss Davis.'

Inez stood with lips drawn tight. She said, 'You needn't make allowances for my beliefs, Mr. Birnes. It really doesn't concern me what you like to think. But I must say you seem strangely eager to discredit the idea of Colin's being able to return.'

Since he made no reply, she continued, 'I would have thought that, being his friend, you would have been only too pleased at the possibility of his being able to get in touch with you again and tell you exactly what had befallen him? Or — is it possible that you don't care to know the facts?'

Deliberately, Birnes turned his back on her and walked towards the windows. Eva looked helplessly at him, then at Inez.

'Don't worry. I'll go, Eva. I've said all I wish to; and so, apparently, has Mr. Birnes. And one thing, darling ... I should advise you to be rather — careful!'

Birnes let that pass too; he didn't want to display his anger in front of Eva; it might have exposed him for what he really was. As it was, he had already been shown in a bad light, and he would have that leeway to make up for now. He listened to Inez leaving without turning his head, then he faced Eva again.

'I can only say I'm sorry. I forgot myself,' he said humbly. 'I should have had more sense as a guest, but I've got the devil's own cussedness when anyone starts talking about spirits existing. I can't stand there and subdue my logicality to that kind of babble.'

Eva smiled faintly. 'You were rather rude to her, but then she gave just as good as she got, I think. She'll get over it in time; it's just her way, and always has been. She doesn't know the meaning of the word tact.'

'I seem to have forgotten that meaning too.' Birnes smiled contritely. 'I hope I haven't caused a row between you two?'

'Oh, no. Inez knows I keep an open mind on spiritualism. She'll not hold that argument with you against me. That wouldn't be at all like her.'

'I'm glad of that,' he told her, patting

her hand gently. 'I should hate to have been the cause of making any trouble for you. I've grown extremely fond of you these last two days, my dear.'

She withdrew her hand, but smiled up. 'I've grown fond of you, Arthur,' she told him. 'In fact, I feel just like your daughter.'

Birnes cursed to himself, but said, 'I may be a great deal older than you in years, Eva, but I don't feel so old. Especially when I'm with you. You rejuvenate me.'

'Is that good?'

He laughed, said, 'I don't quite know. What do you think?'

She let the subject drop, and soon afterwards he took his leave, promising to call her the following day. He went straight home to his rooms, highly satisfied with his progress; Inez's entrance had been a setback, but on the whole he couldn't grumble. His lust for Eva had even driven the apparition he had seemed to see out of his conscience. His high good humour continued as he bathed — continued, in fact, until he chanced to look into the shaving container, and found the map was missing!

9

The Suspicious Jeweller

The Reigate Club in Leicester Square was, as always, quiet and austere that night. It was always quiet and austere — it had a big reputation for being that way. How it managed it in the heart of the Square, no one seemed to know, least of all its exclusive membership. But it did. Big business brains, jaded by the turmoil of a stuffy office, were wont to say: 'Phew! Think I'll bob along to the Club tonight for some peace and quiet,' and when they said that, everyone knew perfectly well they referred only to the Reigate. Even the Senior Conservative had nothing on it for quietness. Members there were at least allowed to cross their legs and sneeze. At the Reigate even this practice was frowned upon.

Its members stole in like the Arabs, and as silently stole away. While inside the

118

club itself they sat stiff and still, the least movement bringing a reproving glare from their fellow clubmen. The aged waiter had brought his talents to bear on the problem of moving like a mouse, and had bested any mouse that ever moved — and also any tortoise.

No papers were read; the rustle would have been distracting. No man ever went to sleep; a member had once been turfed out for snoring in the smoking room, and since then the offence had never been repeated.

But you did get peace and quiet, and a chance to meditate on diverse subjects without being dragged from your thoughts by a pal who wanted a round of snooker with you. The club didn't boast a snooker table.

But this night the place was destined to meet with a rude awakening, and a noisy one. Until the arrival of Arthur Birnes, the old place looked pretty much as usual. Here an ancient member slumped corpse-like in a chair; there another member had removed his shoes to tiptoe out; elsewhere the waiter had just started a half-hour journey to the lounge. A dead and gloomy silence hung about the club, broken only by the furtive scrape of a match in the smoking room. Then Birnes happened.

He happened suddenly and unexpectedly. He was not a Club member, but that didn't deter him. He had been told by George Horton's valet that the wealthy manufacturer of jewellery was at the Reigate Club, and there, in white-hot anger, Birnes had repaired. He had whizzed past the decrepit doorman before that worthy had even seen him coming, and now he was arguing with a waiter at the door of the smoking room.

'I tell you, I must see him. Urgently.'

'But sir, there is a very strict rule . . . '

'*To hell with your rules*. If you don't tell me which room he's in I'll try them all until I find him,' snarled Birnes, his voice resounding through the silence.

'*Ssshhhh!*' hissed a score of voices, and stern glances were bent upon the irate Birnes.

Birnes glared back and snapped, 'Ssshhh, yourselves. Where is he?'

George Horton rose from the depths of a deep armchair and hissed, 'Are you looking for me, Birnes?'

'*There* you are,' snapped Birnes, descending into the room and crossing it with purposeful strides. 'Now, where is it, Horton? I've come to give you one last chance before I turn you in.'

The other members sat up and looked shocked. Horton whispered, 'I don't know what you're talking about, but whatever it is, you haven't any right in this club. If you keep quiet, you'll be all right — if not, you'll get slung out on your neck. Now sit down and try to keep calm.'

Birnes breathed fury and sat; he lowered his voice a little and repeated, 'Where is it, Horton?'

'Where is what? If I had the least idea of what you're driving at, I'd be able to tell you anything I can. But as it is, how can I?'

'You know damn well what I mean,' grated Birnes. '*That map!*'

'Map?'

'Yes, map! Don't pretend you don't

know what I'm driving at, damn you. You're the only one who knew it was in my rooms, the only one who knew what it was worth.'

'But my dear chap, that doesn't say I'd know anything about it. Is it missing or something?'

'Listen,' said Birnes, gripping the table edge until his knuckles showed white. 'Last night you stopped me outside my hotel on a silly pretence of arranging the expedition to Peru. I couldn't think why you'd suddenly changed your mind — until I got upstairs and found my rooms had been searched. Then I realised you must have sent someone after that map; who else could have done so? You had delayed me there outside while your man made his getaway. Isn't that right?'

'It sounds good — go on?'

'So it stands to reason that you're behind this theft which has taken place tonight during my absence.'

'That doesn't follow; and anyway, if you thought someone knew your map was there — if you thought I might be behind an attempt to steal it — why did you leave it there tonight?'

'Because, fool that I was, I assumed that having drawn blank on the first try, you'd think I'd hidden it elsewhere or deposited it in my bank. Whereas it was in my shaving container — and whoever you sent to do your dirty work found that out.'

'In your shaving container? Ingenious little devil, aren't you? And it's gone, has it?'

Birnes seethed. 'I haven't come here to be played with. I'm giving you a chance to hand it over before I call the police in.'

Horton yawned. 'My dear man, you're crazy. Even if I had the map — which I haven't — I wouldn't consider handing it back to you.'

'You're going to,' gritted Birnes between his teeth. 'By God, Horton, if you think I'll stand tamely by and see that map stolen from me after I've as good as murdered — as good as been through hell itself for it, you're wrong.'

Horton's eyes were boring into him now. 'What was that you nearly said, Birnes? You've as good as — murdered for it?'

His words cut through the silence of the room, bringing the other members to their feet suddenly. A score of suspicious eyes were trained on Birnes, and he shrank under them. He mumbled, 'I meant to say, when *I've* as good as *been* murdered for it. Last night, after I'd gone to bed. Someone was hiding behind the curtains in my room, and they tried to — to strangle me.'

Horton stared at him. 'Hiding in your room? Then that accounts for it, you dolt. Whoever was hiding there may have known where it was. Did you hide it, or go to it, last night, not knowing someone was concealed behind the curtains?'

'Why — yes — I did.'

'Then they probably spotted you and returned tonight to collect it in comfort. You simp — you should be more careful, Birnes. I've a damned good mind to have you in court for slander, defamation of character. I've plenty of witnesses here.'

Birnes looked uneasy, murmured, 'I'm sorry, Horton. I didn't stop to think when I found it gone. Everything seemed to point to you.'

'I accept your apology, Birnes. But you want to be more careful in the future. No — don't go yet. I'd like to ask you what you meant exactly by saying you as good as murdered for that map.'

'I didn't — I've told you what I meant to say.'

'So you have. But I don't believe you this time, Birnes. It all fits in with that voice on the phone — the voice which said you had shed blood at Kosan!'

Birnes glanced round furtively, said, 'There's nothing in that, Horton. Nothing. Let it drop.'

'Oh, no, not that fast. You came in here blackening me in front of my fellow members, and unwittingly you put your foot in it, didn't you? Well, now it's my turn to rub it in, and that's what I'm doing. Everyone here knows my record, and everyone knows I'll stoop a bit from the straight and narrow if there's anything in it for me. But murder — that's a horse of a shade I've never seen before. What did you mean when you said you'd murdered for that map?'

Birnes, seized with sudden panic,

unable to answer, suddenly rushed from the room, followed by a multitude of eyes. Within a few seconds he had gone, and shortly after that the Reigate was once more under its pall of graveyard silence.

But Horton was no longer there; Horton had been vaguely suspicious of the mystery surrounding Colin's death from the start. Now he meant to start finding out things. Crook he might be, but the murder of a man brought out some law-abiding streak in his nature. If Birnes was a killer, Horton would do his best to bring him to justice.

★　★　★

'So that's how it is, Miss Davis,' Horton said, draining the glass of whisky she had given him, and staring at her. 'I suspect Birnes of murdering your brother to gain possession of that map.'

Inez Davis was silent; she was also composed. She nodded. 'Does he know you suspect him, Mr. Horton?' she asked.

'He does. I practically accused him of it in front of twenty or thirty witnesses.'

'And what did he answer to that?'

Horton grinned: 'He didn't answer. He ran like he — like the dickens.'

'You've been very kind to come here and tell me this,' said Inez. 'Very kind. I'm most grateful to you for interesting yourself in this affair.'

Horton flushed, said, 'Heck, don't think I'm an officious busybody. I suppose the fact that Birnes has been getting in my hair a lot lately has something to do with my being up against him and coming to you to tell you of my suspicions.'

'Whatever the reason, I'm grateful to you. And I wonder if you would care to help even more and see this — this murderer brought to justice?'

'Anything I can do, within reason,' agreed Horton. 'I'm no angel myself, but when it comes to a dirty tyke like Birnes, I'm more than willing to help fit the noose round his neck.'

'Excellent. Then here's my plan, Mr. Horton . . . ' And she leaned forward and began to tell him her scheme.

★　★　★

'I'm sorry, Mr. Birnes,' said the inspector from the Yard. 'There isn't the least clue to give us a lead. You say the map was valuable?'

'Worth a fortune, man. I must have it back quickly. I risked my life a dozen times for it, Inspector. You just have to do something.'

'We always do our best, sir.' The inspector smiled. 'But in a case like this it's damned awkward. A map. I mean, you might as well say someone had stolen a — a — ' He sought for inspiration, then spoke brightly. ' — a newspaper. If it had been diamonds, or anything of that nature, we might have traced them for you by raiding a few of the better-known fences. But a map . . . '

'Then how about those diamonds which were stolen from me the other day?' rapped Birnes. 'Have you found those yet?'

'I'm afraid not. And God knows we've put a dragnet out for any stones answering to the description you gave. There were rubies and emeralds and topazes amongst them, weren't there?'

'There were, in unusual settings.'

'That's the queer thing; we've search-warranted a number of places where they might have been disposed of, but never a sign of them have we found. I'd say they haven't hit the market yet. It may be the thief is keeping them under cover for a time, sir. They very often do, you know, unless they're pressed for money.'

'Then you haven't a hope of finding this map?'

''Fraid not, sir.'

Birnes snarled, savagely, 'Who the hell claimed 'crime does not pay', with people like you running things for the force?'

The inspector's features hardened. He said tersely, 'That'll be quite sufficient, Mr. Birnes. If you think crime pays, you try it sometime, and you'll see. You always get caught out in the end. If we don't get you, your conscience does.'

He left without another word, without saying 'good afternoon' even, and Birnes was left to think over his parting remark. He was right, damn it! Right! Your conscience did get you — his had got him, and was putting him through hell. It wasn't so much remorse at what he'd done as fear of having to take the consequences. And fear of being driven insane — seeing things like that — that — 'ghost'.

But what could a ghost do? Suppose Colin Davis really was fighting to get a message through from the world to which he had gone? How could it affect Birnes? The English law can't put a spirit on the witness stand — it'd look damned funny, that, a transparent spectre swearing by the Father, Son and Holy Ghost.

Birnes laughed a little at his own wit; that, to him, was the zenith of humour.

No, he hadn't anything to fear, if only he kept his mouth shut and sat tight.

But the map? He couldn't bear to lose that altogether. Not after all he'd done to obtain it. Who could have it? The fiend who'd nearly strangled him in his room? Or had Horton found it after all? Had he just bluffed him that he didn't know anything about it?

He dismissed the entire question to the back of his mind; he couldn't entirely escape feeling disturbed and upset, and wondering what was going to happen next, but he had an appointment with Eva Ferguson for dinner, and he meant to make a big play. It was to be tonight or never, and for his purpose he carried three of the tablets given to him by a Peruvian Indian, which not only made a woman forget, but were reputed to make her the very incarnation of passion.

He opened the door and stepped out — right onto the toes of Inez Davis.

She halted, said quietly, 'The dream has reached an end — I dreamed it through last night!'

10

The Dream

Birnes staggered back into his room; he had scoffed at Inez Davis and her beliefs, but he had been half-afraid of that dream coming to its end. Now, he could see by her eyes that it *had* ended — truthfully.

She walked into the room and stood against the door jamb, her eyes fixed accusingly on his face. He pulled himself together, said, 'And what — what was the end?'

'Don't you know, Mr. Birnes?' Her voice was cold, hostile.

'I? Why should I know? Of course I don't.'

'Then I'll tell you: you remember I'd reached a point where you picked up a rifle and crossed to Colin? You do? Well, in the dream, Mr. Birnes, you struck him across the head with that rifle butt. Then you dragged him through that silent city, left him on the edge of the jungle, senseless — or dead already. Left him for the wild beasts that teem there, and returned to safety yourself. He came to me through the mist again, during the dream. And this time I could see him plainly: blood on his head, face hollow. He spoke. He said, 'Birnes did this — Birnes deserted me.' That was how the dream ended, Mr. Birnes.'

Birnes stood still while the room seemed to whirl about him. His mind was a confused tumult; too many strange things had happened of late, were still happening now.

'What have you to say?' she demanded.

He forced himself to look surprised. 'Say? Nothing. Should I have something to say? You surely aren't going to tell me you believe in that ridiculous dream, are you? Why, Colin and I were the finest of comrades. The suggestion that I'd harm him is so fantastic it's laughable.'

'Just the same, I believe it. I truly believe you struck Colin down and left him lying there, so that you might hold the secret of Kosan entirely to yourself. Or possibly because Colin didn't mean to exploit the riches it held as you would have liked to.'

'That's ridiculous, and if you repeat it you'll be laughed at. I swear I had nothing to do with Colin's fate, whatever it was. Nor can you prove I did.'

'No, I can't prove anything, can I? But I thought you'd like to know that at least one person believes you guilty of a filthy trick.'

Birnes shrugged, said, 'Thank you for telling me; now I know just where I stand with you. And now, if you've no objections, I'm late for an appointment.'

'With Eva?'

'That need not concern you. And if you venture to repeat your foolish suspicions to anyone, Miss Davis, I will decidedly take action against you. Good night.'

She gave him a look which made his heart thud with uneasiness. Then she turned her back on him and walked from the room. He followed more leisurely, and when he reached the street and his taxi, she had gone.

He gave the driver Eva Ferguson's address, and was rapidly whisked across town and decanted outside her residence.

She welcomed him pleasantly, and he knew that Inez had not been on the telephone to her about the dream, for she did not refer to it over dinner. Her father was still out of town, and most of the servants were taking their night off. There was only the cook and an old maid in the house, and they were somewhere in the scullery regions with instructions not to disturb Miss Eva and her visitor.

Birnes could not have planned things better himself. So many worries were crowding in on him that he felt, if he left the conquest much longer, he would be too sick in mind to carry it through. He felt the reassuring roundness of the tablets in his pocket, and gazed amorously at his intended victim.

Eva was prattling of this and that, naturally. Apparently she was not aware of any strain in the atmosphere; Birnes didn't seem out of the normal to her. She couldn't, of course, know how his pulse raced and his heart thudded with excitement when he watched the way her green silk dress clung to her. She brought drinks and set them on an occasional table in front of the settee. She poured them, smiling at him.

'By the way, my dear, I wonder if you happen to have a set of encyclopaedias handy? There's a little item about Peru that I'd like to look up.'

'Why, yes, Father has the Britannica in his study. I'll get it for you, shall I?'

'Just the volume including P, if it isn't too much trouble.'

She nodded and went out, and Birnes waited until her footsteps died away down the hall. Then he brought out the tablets and slipped two into her drink, quickly stirring them with his fingers for want of anything better.

By the time she came back he was sitting comfortably on the divan, and the tablets had dissolved altogether. She handed him the green-bound volume, and he flicked pages until he found Peru, then made a pretence of reading the article.

He watched her from the corner of his eye; her drink was nearly finished, and already a languorous drowsiness was creeping over her. A few more minutes and the time would be ripe; she would forget who she was, where she was, in the grip of the exotic drug.

It was happening already; he had laid aside the book, and she was looking at him through half-closed eyelids, her body relaxed and leaning against his. Now she sighed and allowed herself to fall even more heavily upon him. He shifted his position, placed an arm about her waist, said, 'If you're tired, dear, why not lie down on here for a while?'

She nodded without speaking, and he moved again so that he could lay her gently down on the divan. She sighed, and her arms wound about his neck: tightly, passionately.

Now!

His own hands came towards her, his lips parted, eyes gleaming; and as he stooped over her, he chanced to glimpse the window behind.

With a cry of terror he reeled back from the divan; there was a face there again — Colin's face, still bloodstained, still menacing.

'Oh, God,' mumbled Birnes to himself,

his hands clenched tightly together. 'I'm not seeing things — it *is* there. It *must* be there.'

But when he looked again, it had gone.

He paced up and down the room, ignoring the now-sleeping girl on the divan. He was going mad; he must be going mad. The thing he had done out there had unhinged his mind, and everything that happened sprang from his mental state. But no — that strangling episode during the night hadn't been any mental affliction. He still had faint bruises round his throat even now.

A tap at the door made him almost jump out of his skin; it opened and the maid looked in.

'Doctor Gorse to see you, madam,' she began; then said, 'Oh!'

'She's asleep,' grated Birnes. 'Tell the doctor to call some other time.'

A burly figure pushed past the maid; a gruff, hearty voice said, 'Asleep, is she? Well, we'll soon alter that.'

'What the devil d'you mean by bursting in here?' demanded Birnes, angrily. 'I told the maid to tell you . . . '

'Yes, yes, yes,' said Doctor Gorse testily. 'I know what you told the maid. But I wish to see Miss Ferguson, and I intend to.'

'But you've no right . . . '

'When you've doctored a family as long as I have this one, young man, you've a lot of rights that you wouldn't have in the ordinary way. Hello — funny. This isn't a natural sleep. Why, bless my soul, if I didn't know any better I'd say she'd been taking drugs!'

'What?' Birnes tried to convey surprise, but didn't do it too well. 'Drugged, you say, Doctor?'

'Yes.' Gorse looked curiously at the other man, noted his white face, trembling hands, 'I wonder how that happened?'

'I — I've no idea. She — she just went to sleep while I was glancing at an article in the encyclopaedia, and I didn't like to wake her.'

'Strange, that. She called on me this morning to tell me that worrying about her fiancé was making it impossible for her to sleep at all. I decided to slip round tonight and give her some sleeping tablets

— but apparently someone's beaten me to it, eh?'

Birnes stammered, 'I — I can't understand. I didn't know she was in — in the habit of taking drugs.'

'Nor did I. But it seems fairly obvious, doesn't it? Anyway, we can ask her about it when she recovers, and meanwhile I think I'd better stay with her.'

'As you wish,' grunted Birnes. He sat down and tried to look calm and collected. Gorse was still eyeing him keenly. He said, 'Why the devil are you staring at me like that?'

'Was I? I beg your pardon. Your face interests me — the expression of it. You look like a man afflicted by some tremendous problem — a man whose nerves are shot to pieces.'

'I am,' said Birnes. The urge to confide in someone, and seek sympathy, was rising strongly in him. He went on, 'Do you believe in ghosts, Doctor?'

'Stuff and nonsense.'

'That's what I thought, until tonight. But — I saw one — not ten minutes ago. At that window.'

'You what?'

'It's true. I couldn't have imagined it so plainly, Doctor. Or could I?'

'You certainly could. In fact, I wouldn't believe anything else but that you *did* imagine it. Was it a ghost you knew, or just any old ghost?'

His tone was jocular, but with a serious note in it. Birnes said, 'I knew the man in life. He was — well, my employer, in one respect. He was — he vanished in a lost city we discovered. It was Miss Ferguson's fiancé, Colin Davis.'

'And the matter has weighed heavily on your mind?'

'Very heavily.'

'Then there's your answer,' said the doctor. 'You must not allow yourself to think of it at all. Clear the past from your life — the ghost you saw is only in your own brain. That's good advice, young man, and if I were giving it to you professionally it would cost you two guineas. See that you take it.'

'Thanks,' said Birnes. 'You're probably right, and I will.'

But, as if to give the lie to the doctor's

words, his eyes even at that moment focused on the window — and once again the white face of Colin Davis was pictured there!

'Look!' he almost screamed. 'Doctor — there — outside.'

Gorse whirled quickly, but his face remained blank.

'There — damn you, can't you see it? Right in the centre. Staring — staring — get it away from there — it'll drive me mad! Get it away!'

'Steady, man — steady yourself.'

Birnes was sunk back against the upholstery of his chair, his features twisted with fear, his breath rasping harshly from livid lips. Gorse snapped, 'Get hold of yourself. There's nothing there. It's in your imagination. The window is perfectly blank.'

Slowly, Birnes' terror evaporated. Dully, he said, 'Now it's gone again. Didn't you — see it?'

'I saw nothing. As I've told you, it's entirely your mind that causes this trouble. You're worrying unduly.'

'You mean — I'm — I'm mad?'

'Nothing of the kind. I mean that you

aren't quite rational at the moment. You're suffering from a distressing mental condition which is akin to a persecution complex.'

'I see.'

Birnes sat drinking heavily while the minutes ticked away; he wanted to get up, get out, go home, but he felt his legs would not have carried him. Dismiss it from his mind? The old fool. How could anyone dismiss a thing like that from their mind? It was too real, too frightening. But then again, the old doctor didn't know what he had on his conscience. What had the police inspector said? 'If we don't get you — your conscience does!'

He was right about that. Birnes realised his conscience had got him. The trouble was, where was it going to end; when?

'She's coming to,' said Doctor Gorse.

'Eh?'

Birnes snapped out of his reverie, to see that Eva was breathing more normally, and that her eyelids were flickering. He knew the drug's effects lasted for the better part of an hour, and that it left the victim with only a hazy idea of what had taken place previously to its administration. He was not worried about what Eva might have to say. She could not accuse him of anything.

'There we are,' said Gorse, gently, helping her to sit up. 'How do you feel?'

'Fine, apart from a slight headache,' she answered faintly. 'But what happened to me? Doctor — why are you here? Did I faint?'

'I'm sure you didn't. I should say you were under the effect of some drug or other. You — didn't take it yourself, did you?'

'Of course I didn't. I hadn't any drugs to take, Doctor. You must be wrong, surely.'

'I may be. But I don't think I am. However, if you say you took no drug, possibly it was administered to you without your knowledge? Is this your glass here?' He picked up the empty glass, and she nodded. Birnes suddenly started to sweat. Gorse was about to say something else, when the door opened again — and Inez Davis, George Horton, and a stout lady in purple velvet walked in!

11

The Materialization

Birnes' head spun as he gazed at them. Inez Davis and George Horton — the two people who had strong suspicions of him. What were they doing together? What were they doing here?

He soon had the answer to that: Inez spoke almost at once, before anyone else had had time to. She said, 'Hello, Eva — Doctor Gorse, and — Mr. Birnes. May I introduce the people with me? Madame English, the well-known West End medium; and Mr. Horton, the jeweller. Both of them have kindly consented to help tonight.'

'Help? Help in what?' demanded Eva, and Birnes stiffened in his chair.

'The seance,' said Inez calmly. 'I've decided it's the only way to put my mind at rest. We must hold a seance here, and try to get in touch with poor Colin. You don't mind, Eva?'

Doctor Gorse stepped forward. 'Do you think it's advisable at the moment? Miss Ferguson has — not been too well, and Mr. Birnes is also distressed mentally.'

'I don't mind,' said Eva. 'Frankly, Inez, I think you're wasting your time, but if it'll set your mind at rest, I'm game.'

'How about you, Mr. Birnes?' said Inez, coldly.

'I — I have to go — I'm sorry.'

'It's no good without 'im, love,' said Madame English. 'Nowt'll come through.'

She spoke with a strong Lancashire accent, and Gorse smiled.

'You see, Mr. Birnes,' Inez continued, 'you're indispensable as the last person to see Colin alive, and also as his best friend. You will stay?'

'I can't. I'm sorry.'

'You aren't — afraid, are you?'

'I resent that — you're always making implications, Miss Davis.'

'Then, if you haven't anything to be afraid of, why not spare us half an hour? Let's clear the thing up one way or the other. Let's get Colin back to speak to us.'

'I wouldn't subject myself to any such foolish tricks,' said Birnes.

'They aren't foolish, young feller-me-lad,' sniffed the Madame. ''E'll come back all reet if you concentrate 'ard enough.'

'Yes, come on, Birnes,' put in Horton. 'What are you scared of, man?'

There wasn't really much choice for Birnes. If he refused to take part in the seance, he would rouse deeper suspicion than ever. After all, if he had nothing to fear, why be afraid?

He mumbled, 'Very well. I still think it foolish, but I'll stay.'

'Good,' said Inez, briskly. 'I hope you'll stay too, Doctor. It may be interesting. And now, Madame English, if you'll arrange things as you want them, we'll get on with the seance so that Mr. Birnes may keep his other engagement.'

Madame English nodded, and bustled about drawing a table to the centre of the room and arranging chairs round it. That done, she put out all the lights except the red-shaded reading lamp, which she turned down low on its stand, so that the strength of the light was directed to the floor. She stood back and approved her handiwork.

'That's about it, love,' she told Inez. 'Now, if you'd all teck your seats, we'll manage champion. Just sit straight an' put 'ands on't table top, fingers touching — and whatever you do, don't break t'circle. It'd be dangerous to me.'

She beamed at them and they sat down. Birnes was the last to take his place, in between Horton and Gorse, facing the windows.

'Now,' said Madame English, impressively, 'I'll sit 'ere at th'ead o't table — eeh, it's a reet tight squeeze, isn't it? Bit too congested, it is. Never fret, loves, we'll manage all reet.'

She inserted her large bulk into a high-backed chair and puffed relief. Once in position, she said, 'Now, ah'll 'ave to ask you all t' concentrate on't chap as you want bringing back. Colin, 'is name is, isn't it? Aye. Don't get excited, loves, it'll be reet. You won't move nor stir once ah've gone int't trance. Now, 'ere goes.'

Her already unlovely features twisted into a ferocious scowl. Her eyes closed.

When next she spoke, the Lancashire twang was hardly noticeable. She looked impressive and dignified sitting there, waiting for the spirits to come through to her.

'They're restless tonight,' she intoned, as a shudder shook her ample frame. 'They all want to speak — concentrate hard, please. Concentrate!'

The others sat motionless, their minds forced on to Colin. Birnes didn't want to think of him, but he couldn't help himself. He was scared half out of his wits, and getting more frightened every second. Suppose there should be anything in all this? Obviously the fat medium believed — he couldn't imagine any duplicity in her.

And then she said, jerkily, 'He's coming — I can feel him. He's answering the call. He's coming — nearer — nearer — nearer — '

And Birnes suddenly sprang to his feet with a terrified cry! His eyes were staring fixedly towards the window. Out there he could see a pallid-faced spectre, drawing closer across the lawn, carrying in its hand the ancient sacrificial knife of the

Incas which Colin had taken from the victim on that altar in the temple of the Sun God in Kosan!

Nearer, nearer it came, and Birnes cringed away towards the far wall, shrieking, shrieking.

The séance had stopped; the rest were crowding about the crazed man, trying to soothe him. But he would not be soothed.

He said, frantically, '*Stop him*. He's coming — he's *coming for me!* Don't let him touch me . . . stop him. Look! Can't you *see?* There — coming in through the window. He's here, I tell you!'

'Calm down, man,' said Gorse. 'He won't harm you. He's in your imagination.'

'He *isn't*,' said Madame English quietly. 'He's here, in this room, I can feel it. And he's angry — *angry* — '

'With *me*,' babbled Birnes. 'I — I struck him down while he was sleeping in Kosan — and left him without weapons or food. He'll kill me — he's coming nearer.'

And, with a last despairing shriek, Birnes fainted . . .

Slowly, he came up from the hell he had been in. His eyes opened and he glanced round. They were still here, all of them. But now they had been joined by a uniformed constable and a plain-clothes man.

He realized with a start that he was handcuffed!

And standing before him, wiping a red stain from his forehead, was Colin Davis!

Colin, whom he had last seen lying senseless in the jungle at Kosan. Colin, not dead, but very much alive.

'He's come round,' said Horton, and all eyes were turned on the wretched Birnes.

'What — what does this mean?' stuttered Birnes, fearfully.

Colin stepped forward, looked at him grimly.

'It means a nice long spell in jail for you, Birnes,' he rapped. 'For attempted murder!'

'But — you can't prove . . . '

'We've enough proof here,' said Inez. 'Enough witnesses to put you away. We all heard your confession.'

Birnes groaned and sunk his head on his hands. Then he looked up, said, 'At least you haven't got the map, Davis!'

'You're wrong. I have. It was *I* who took it from your apartment. It was *I* who half-strangled you that night. I stole the gems you left lying about, and I was the voice on the telephone, and the man who wrote the note warning you. *It was all me*, Birnes.'

'But — but how did you escape? The — the animals?'

'Never penetrated so near to the lost city,' supplied Colin. 'If you hadn't been in such a state, you'd have remembered how there never seemed to be any animals about there. You remarked on it. I don't know how long I was senseless after your blow, but when I came round it was daylight. You'd taken everything. I can't begin to say how I made it, but armed with only an ornamental axe, an Inca sword, and a knife, I somehow did manage to get back to the nearest outpost where I could get help.

'While you loafed about on your

journey home, I flew back, and prepared all this especially for your benefit. I knew I could never hope to prove anything against you myself; I had to think out some way of playing on your conscience so much that you'd break down and confess. It worked, Birnes.'

'You mean — everything was — was *arranged*?'

'Everything. Even while you were breaking your sad news to Eva, she knew all the time that you'd really tried to kill me. I must say, both Eva and Inez acted damn well — and so did you, Doctor Gorse, thank you.'

'Horton. Was he in on it?'

'No, he wasn't. Not until the last minute. We enlisted him because he suspected you himself, and because you knew he did, and that would be one more factor to unsettle you.'

Birnes groaned, said, 'I'm sorry about it all, Colin. I haven't had a minute's sleep since it happened. You — you aren't going to turn me in — are you?'

'I am. I think you'd be best out of the way for a few years. I don't know what you'll get for attempted murder, but it ought to be pretty stiff. Sorry, and all that, but that trek back to civilization, with my life in danger every minute, kind of made me feel nastier than I used to do. I think you can take him now, officers.'

The constable hoisted Birnes to his feet and jerked him along out of the room. His conscience wouldn't trouble him any more — but other things would.

When he had gone, Horton said, 'It's been nice knowing you people, and helping. Glad he's been put away. There's just one thing: is there really anything in this spiritualism business?'

'I don't know.' Colin smiled. 'But if there is, Inez certainly doesn't believe in the supernatural; do you, dear? She's the most natural girl I know, bar none. Birnes might have known that, if he'd glanced at the bills outside the Round Theatre and seen her name there. Might even have guessed our delightful Madame English was another of the cast.'

'I enjoyed doing it immensely.' Madame smiled. 'Except that I do abhor this horrible purple effusion.'

Inez said, 'Well, George has asked me to go along and look at his etchings, Colin. So I think I'll buzz off.' They said good night, and she and Horton, arms linked, left the house. Gorse and Madame English followed them, leaving Colin and Eva alone.

'Colin, I'm so glad it worked out so well. I don't know where I'd have turned if you hadn't ever come back.'

'Don't worry again, darling.' He grinned, taking her in his arms. 'I'm through with all that — someone else can investigate Kosan. Personally, right now, I'm more interested in investigating married life!'

And there was nothing very ghostly about his kiss!

The Frightened Girl

1

Girl Grabs Boy

The café was crowded. Although it was long past midnight, a couple of hundred people sat at the tables. Men and women of all professions and of almost all countries were there, some animated, vivacious, others worn out and sleepy. The cosmopolitan crowd which throngs the centre of London's West End seemed to have selected from its people a representative sample and sent them into this café. Yet Danny King could not see, among all those present, the man he had come to meet.

Danny sat at a corner table from where he could see right across the café. A newspaper was held conveniently near at hand so that he could cover his interest when it aroused curiosity among the people he observed. As he scanned the faces of the men entering, there flashed across his mind the description he had been given at the Yard of the man he was to meet. 'About six feet; aged about thirty; full, round face; fair hair; scar on cheek. Powerful build. This man is armed.'

There had been other details, but Danny King needed only these to pick his man from a crowd. 'It might be myself, scar and all,' he mused as he fingered the souvenir of a razor-gang slashing on his cheek.

'Is this anybody's seat?'

The voice made him switch his gaze from the door to the young woman who, holding the empty chair with one hand, was offering to sit at his table. Danny had a quick glimpse of thick, copper-coloured hair and full red lips as he shook his head in reply and went back to watching the newcomers with a more guarded scrutiny. He soon became absorbed again in his search.

'You're waiting for someone?' The girl's voice contained an accusation. Danny switched his eyes from the door and looked at the girl with so puzzled an air that she laughed.

'Oh, I'm sorry,' she said. 'I guess it isn't any of my business.'

'It isn't,' Danny said, and raised his paper, preparing to read but keeping his eye on the door. The girl was uncommonly pretty, and this made him all the more determined to be sharp with her. Pretty girls, from Danny King's point of view, made too much use of their good looks. They could be dangerous.

'You see, if you were expecting someone I wouldn't sit right here,' the girl went on, refusing to be crushed, 'because I'd be taking her place, wouldn't I?' Her voice sounded like a bright child's as she put the final question.

Danny glared at her. 'Look, Mabel or Daisy or whatever your name is, whatever it is you've got, I don't want it, so you're wasting your time. I'm just an ordinary fellow with no dough and no ideas about women, so beat it.'

The girl's blue eyes flashed. She looked so hurt and taken aback that Danny began to feel sorry. Maybe he'd made a mistake. All kinds of women got into these cafés at night and most of them were touting for clubs or drinking dens or other shady places, or simply on the lookout for a sucker.

Her ruby lips curled.

'Just a big wide-awake city slicker and want everyone to know it, huh?' the girl said. 'Well you're wrong this time, Mr. Slicker, because I'm not the sort you take me for, and if I was, I'm sure I wouldn't waste my time on a broken-down, untidy, sloppy twerp.'

This attack jolted Danny. He hid behind his paper for a moment. Having absorbed the girl's insults and the bitter tone in which they were delivered, he put the paper down and said,

'Now, see here, I didn't mean anything. I'm just an ordinary feller working all day and I'm too busy to talk. That's all. So lay off the conversation, will you? I'm pretty busy all day and I've got to catch up on my reading.'

'Then why don't you put your paper the right way up?' the girl asked. Danny's paper stopped rising to its position in front of his nose, and he stared at it.

Then, reversing it quickly, he caught the girl's eyes. They were twinkling with mischievous laughter and it got Danny.

He laughed shortly. 'Can't you let a fellow alone?' He had recovered his good humour. 'Here I am,' he went on, 'sitting here, minding my own business, and you come along and bawl me out just because my paper's upside down.' At this one-sided, grotesque description of the situation they both laughed again. The girl, Danny decided, was even prettier when she laughed. Her face grew serious and she bent forward.

'*Talk* to me, please,' she said urgently. 'Talk to me as if you'd known me all my life. Pretend that you are here with me, as if you'd brought me here. *Please!* I'm in trouble — desperate trouble.'

In spite of himself Danny was taken aback.

'Why?' he asked.

'I can't tell you,' she said. 'That is, it's all so silly that you wouldn't believe it even if I told you. And it's all so involved. But, you see, there's a man and he's — he's after me. I'm afraid that if he sees me in here by myself I shall, I mean, he'll come up and try to — to hurt me,' she finished lamely, trying to make her story convincing yet half-realising that she was failing.

But Danny nodded sympathetically. 'I see,' he said, 'and you think that if he sees you and me talking he'll leave you alone, huh?' He paused as the girl nodded, and then went on, 'Aha, I think I can see someone looking at you.'

The girl froze and a look of terror came into her blue eyes.

'Is he a tall man with a red beard and one eye, wearing a cutlass and a three-cornered hat with a skull-and-crossbones on it?' Danny asked.

'So you *don't* believe me!' the girl said. 'I *knew* you wouldn't. Oh, it's not a bit of good trying to explain, but *do please* try to believe me. I'm in a horrible jam and all you need to do is to talk to me. Just keep on talking like you're doing now.'

Danny King came to the conclusion that his quarry wouldn't turn up. He'd been waiting there for a long time, and already the stranger he was to meet was an hour and a half late. Besides, the look that had flashed through the girl's eyes had been one of real terror. Danny King had seen that look on the faces of many people, sometimes written large over the whole features and sometimes a mere flash behind the eyes. He knew that whether the girl's story was true or false, she was badly scared of something. He smiled at her humanly.

'O.K.,' he said. 'Let's talk, shall we? Suppose we start by telling each other our names. Mine's Danny, and you can have the surname King for good measure. What's your name?'

The girl's eyelids dropped. Studying her long eyelashes and her soft, full-coloured cheeks, Danny thought, *Here comes the good old alias.*

'Sandra's my name,' the girl said. 'Sandra Mason.' The name slid through Danny's mind. So certain was he that it was false that he made no effort to remember it.

'You know,' he said, grinning, 'I knew a girl once who told me her name was Cherry Smith. That was O.K. until I looked at her bank book and found it belonged to Mabel Jones. But that isn't all. Her father's name was Robinson and all her friends called her Molly.'

The girl coloured and snapped at him, 'You make me *mad*. You're simply a smart city slicker. You don't believe anything you hear, do you, smart guy?'

'Lady,' Danny said, 'do I look like a city slicker or a smart guy?' He smoothed his rough, wiry hair down and pulled his coat around him tightly into his body so that it was waisted, trying his best to look the part.

The girl laughed. 'You look rather nice,' she said. 'In fact — '

'In fact, that's why you came and sat down here,' Danny accused. 'You said, 'There's a nice young edition of the real old English gentleman', and so you decided to plunge on me rather than that fat, stupid-looking man over there.'

The girl looked round and then gave a start. Danny was quick to follow her gaze by the tilt of her head but he saw nothing, nor anyone, unusual. The girl turned back to him and began talking with forced animation.

'Do you often come here?' she began, but broke off when she saw Danny was still trying to see what had made her start. She stopped, and then began again. 'Please, you've got to help me! I'm in real trouble, and if you won't help I shall have to find someone who will. Besides, it's a lot worse now. I've got to leave this dive, and I daren't without someone to help me. If I go out of here by myself, they — I mean, *he* — will catch me. I'm in dreadful danger, really I am.'

'Let's get this quite straight, lady,' Danny said. 'You're in danger. Right?' He began to count the items off on his fingers, one by one. 'There's a *man* or *some men* after you. Right? If they see you here alone, *he*, or *they*, will molest you. Right? And if you leave here alone, he, or they, will follow you and molest you. *Right . . . ?* Now, sweetheart, if you want my help, all I can do is to give you some advice, and that is this: call the waiter, tell him you want a policeman because you're afraid of someone molesting you, and then wait for the bobby to turn up in the foyer outside. And if you

167

can't do that, then my next advice is, give up reading mystery stories. They're too exciting for you. That damsel-in-distress gag is antique.'

If he had expected any fight back from the girl, he was mistaken. She leaned back in her chair and heaved a weary sigh, running her hand across her forehead. Danny noted that she was stylishly and expensively dressed, and the wristlet watch she looked at so anxiously was an expensive item. She caught his eye upon her watch, and with a sudden movement, she ripped it off her wrist.

'*Here*,' she said, a bitter twist to her mouth and scorn in her voice. 'I'll make it worth your while. This watch is worth *something*, isn't it? If you'll take me home, I'll give it to you. Here, *take it*. All I want you to do is to take me out of here and find me a cab and just take me home. I'll pay the fare.'

'But suppose your man — or men — follows?' Danny objected. 'Will you be all that safe at home?'

The girl gave a short laugh. 'I don't need a watchdog, Romeo,' she said. 'Only an escort. Well, will you do it?'

Danny stood up. He brushed aside the watch and beckoned the waiter for his bill. 'Sure I'll come,' he said impulsively. Together he and the girl made for the café door. Something was in the air, Danny knew. All the signs pointed to what he called 'a small slice of excitement', and it was on these small slices that he lived. He was one of the youngest of the Special Branch men of the C.I.D. and yet he was already a veteran. And now a sixth sense which had stood him in good stead in many a tight corner warned him of a danger lurking somewhere. He paid his bill at the cash desk and linked arms with the girl as, together, they left the café.

Danny was on the lookout for a taxi and for a possible trailer or lurker in the shadows. But he saw nothing. He asked his companion and received an address in Maida Vale. Together they walked in silence across the Circus and down Piccadilly itself. The girl was rigid at his side, nor did she speak, and Danny felt his sense of danger still with him. It was with relief that he saw ahead the dim lights of a cruising taxi, and he hailed it. The taxi came abreast of him and stopped; the driver leaned out to hear the address Danny shouted. Suddenly the girl, who was standing behind him, cried out in fear; Danny turned to catch a glimpse of her running fast up the street.

'*Hey!*' he shouted and a heavy blow from behind struck him on the head as a strong grip seized his arms and a hand clamped down on his mouth. Dazed and struggling, he was lifted into the taxi.

2

Just Off Piccadilly

Danny could tell by the way he was being handled that he had two men to deal with. At first surprise had made him struggle, but now he began to relax, and pretended that the blow on the back of his head had indeed knocked him out. Dazed and shaken, he allowed his captors to pull him into the cab and heard one of them shout to the driver to drive on. Danny lay on the floor of the cab propped up against the back seat, his face turned up, his eyes closed. He was getting back his wind and behind the blank, unconscious look, his mind was working furiously.

'*Strewth!*' one of his captors exclaimed as a light flashed on Danny's face. 'This ain't him. We've coshed the wrong bloke.'

'Garn,' the other said, and then Danny heard him curse savagely. 'It ain't neither.

Why, the cunning little witch! Where'd she dig this feller up?'

'Darned if I know. Either she never meant to meet Juke tonight or else she used this feller to fool us. I wonder what he knows about it all. Wake him up, will you?'

The other began slapping Danny's face vigorously, and Danny opened his eyes. He did not try to struggle up, but began to shout instead.

'Not so much ruddy row,' said one of his captors. 'Not a peep out of place from you, see, or you'll get *this* on the other side of your face.' He showed Danny an enormous fist, holding it close up to his face in a manner which aroused all of Danny's fighting ire.

'And if you don't want a good hiding, cocker, talk up fast and lively, see,' the other said. 'And don't try no funny stuff.'

Danny thought savagely of how he'd like to try some funny stuff himself on these two hooligans, and how he'd wipe the bullying smile off their faces merely by showing his official pass. But he wanted to know why he had been kidnapped and carried off, and what part the girl played in the whole affair. With this in mind, he sat still and said nothing, but looked from one to the other of the two toughs with what he hoped was a terrified air. At last he managed to break out with:

'What — whatever happened? Who are you, and how dare you assault me?'

'Nah, look here, young feller-me-lad,' said one of the toughs, bunching Danny's shirt front up into a big fistful and pushing his ugly face close to the young man's. 'Don't try none of the free-and-easy innocent stuff with us. What was you doing with the Stammers Judy, and how came you to get yourself into making a fool out of us?'

Danny thought for a moment before replying. He was surprised to find that the girl had been telling the truth. What he wanted very much to know was: had she deliberately lured him away from the café?

'I don't understand you,' he said. 'I've never seen the young lady before in my life.'

The tough who was holding Danny's shirt began to shake him and curse him fluently, but the other stopped him.

''Arf-a-mo, 'arf-a-mo, Nobby,' he said. 'Let's ask the mug how he comes to be with the Judy. Now,' he said, addressing Danny, 'let's have it straight. I know when you're lying, mind, and if I think you are, Nobby here'll have your blinking liver out in two ticks.'

'Very well then,' Danny said. 'If you want to know, this is it.' He briefly described how the girl had come up to him in the café and had asked him to escort her home.

The thugs listened, open-mouthed.

'You say you ain't never seen the dame before?' said Nobby. 'An' yet you undertakes to go home with her, knowing full well you might get done in?'

'Never thought she was telling the truth for a moment,' Danny said. 'I reckoned she was exaggerating.'

He saw the other man was listening intently to his story, nodding his head as if in agreement.

''S'right, Nobby,' he said. 'This bird

has been fooled just the same as we have. Now look here, mister, you bit off just a little more than you could chew tonight, and a bit more than that as well. I ain't sorry I coshed you, because you weren't keeping your nose clean anyway. So just you forget about this and don't go talking about it, see, or it'll be the worse for you. And don't forget this — no coppers. Keep away from the police and you'll be O.K. And if you meet with a strange dame again, keep your nose clean.' He said to his companion, 'O.K., Nobby. Tell Tish to stop and dump this guy.'

Nobby spoke to the driver and the cab slowed to a stop.

'Just a minute,' Danny spoke from the floor. 'I've got a thing or two to say to you fellows before I leave you. You aren't the only ones who need to keep your noses clean.'

He saw Nobby snarl and heard the door open. Danny's two hands closed round Nobby's foot and Danny rose from the floor, lifting the whole leg and twisting so that the tough was thrown off the seat.

Releasing his hold on the foot when it was chest-high, Danny swung a flailing chopper stroke with the heel of his palm at the other tough who was moving in to grapple him. The blow landed on the man's throat, right in his Adam's apple, and he began to splutter and choke, his legs thrashing in agony.

The driver, who had supposed the sounds of combat to be his two friends beating up their victim, had not turned round, nor did he show any great surprise until Danny sprang from the cab and hit him a smashing right on the point of the jaw, knocking him out so that he slumped over the wheel. Then the young man turned to deal with the tough called Nobby, who was emerging from the cab to avenge himself.

As the man sprang to the pavement Danny hit him with a body blow on the solar plexus and the big man collapsed with a wheezing groan. In a flash Danny had his handcuffs out and round the wrists of the two spluttering toughs.

The driver of the cab was still unconscious and was slumped over the wheel. Just across the road Danny could make out the rectangular lines of a telephone kiosk. In less than a minute he was on the phone to the Yard, and soon after a wagon was on its way to pick up his three captives.

When he got back to the taxi, he found the two toughs had recovered themselves and were staring stupidly at the handcuffs around their wrists. The driver, too, was beginning to moan and groan as he struggled to regain consciousness.

'Cor,' said the tough called Nobby. 'A blinking flattie. The cunning witch; she set a flattie on us, Mac.'

Mac looked savagely at Danny. 'You might have got us this time, you damn copper,' he gritted out. 'But you won't get away with it.'

Danny King grinned at them benevolently.

'Funny how things turn out, isn't it?' he said.

'What have you done with Juke?' Nobby whined. 'I suppose he split — ow!' He broke off quickly as the other tough kicked his shin.

'Oh yes, everything will be taken down and used in evidence against you,' Danny said pleasantly. 'You're quite right, Mac, to shut up your talkative friend.' At that moment the police van arrived.

'Evening, Sergeant,' Danny said as the policeman approached and shone his torch upon the ground around the taxi. 'D'you recognize any of 'em?'

'Can't say I do, Mr. King,' the sergeant said. 'We'll check up at the station.'

★　★　★

Some hours later Danny King was seated at a conference table at Scotland Yard. The man at the head of the table was none other than Sir James Blair, head of the Big Five.

'These two men both have records for petty offences, mostly connected with the docks,' Sir James said. 'Neither will tell us much, and that indicates they are well paid by some organization. They stick to their story that they were asked by the girl, by way of a joke, to kidnap her companion. Until we find this girl we can't disprove this statement. But King says that, from the conversation which passed between the two men in the cab, they were in fact not hired by the girl for any purpose whatsoever. Is that correct, King?'

'That's fairly definite, sir,' Danny said. 'The girl's fear was obviously genuine. She knew that someone was after her, and it's my belief that she would have been caught as well as me if she hadn't run for it. The only other thing that occurs to me is that these two men knew I was trying to contact the man who calls himself Sid Jones. For some reason they wanted to stop me meeting him. They must have known that I would go to his lodgings when he didn't show up. But there's just one screwy thing. These two fellows, from their talk, expected someone different from me to be with the girl. That's what doesn't make sense. Who were they after, and why? And how does this girl fit in? I'm sure that this girl, the two fellows who nabbed me, and the mysterious Sid Jones all fit together. The key to the whole thing is the girl. Find her, and you've got the case broken right open.'

'We've got the dragnet out,' another detective said. 'Records say that there are one or two on the cards who answer to Danny's description, and we expect to get a pretty good parade for him by this evening.'

'Well,' Sir James said, 'the people we are up against are a smart crew. They must have known that this man Jones had agreed to contact King here. That seems obvious because the man didn't show up. But whether this girl has anything to do with their smuggling activities, we don't know. We've got two petty dock thieves with small records. We can't link them up with the gang. We know from the conversation King heard that they are connected with the girl. So whether you think — as King does — that the whole thing links up; or whether you tend to the view that the mysterious Sid Jones, and the girl and her rough playmates, are two separate items, you must face the fact that we are now no further than we were before.

'We still don't know when or where this

boat with its cargo of guns is reaching England. And unless we find that out and strike, every gangster, every sneak thief, every burglar in England will be armed. We've got to smash this organization, gentlemen, before it's too late. We nearly did it when the man Jones decided to confess and arranged to meet King. But now he hasn't shown up. We were relying on this man because he was the one person whom we actually knew was engaged in smuggling arms into this country.'

Sir James faced his Scotland Yard men fiercely. 'Gentlemen, the matter is serious. It merits the immediate attention and urgent cooperation of all departments. Luckily we have Jones's address, and enquiries have already been made. But we must act quickly.'

Sir James sat down and, amid a buzz of conversation, the conference broke up. Danny King walked from the large room, deep in thought. He had a hunch that was more than a hunch that the girl he had met was in some way connected with the gang of gun-runners he was trying to track down. But how to find her?

He plunged his hands in his pockets, and then stopped suddenly. He let out a loud whistle and drew an object from his pocket, holding it in the palm of his hand.

The girl's watch! So she *had* been determined he should have it. She must have slipped it into his pocket. Well, that was as good a clue as any.

He turned the watch over. On the back was engraved: *To Sandra. Love K.*

He placed the watch back into his pocket, and went off through the corridors of Scotland Yard until he found the man he wanted.

'You won't have much trouble in tracing this,' the expert said. 'It's not a very common make, and the vendor's mark is English. If I were you, I'd try — ' He mentioned a famous Bond Street jeweller's.

'Thanks,' Danny said. 'I will.' He replaced the watch in his pocket and went out. He had barely reached the hall on the ground floor when he heard his name being called. A police clerk was running after him.

'Oh, Mr. King,' the clerk said, 'you're wanted on the phone. And Davidson says will you please hold it, as they're trying to pick the fellow up before he leaves the call-box? They've traced the call already.'

'O.K.' In a flash Danny was in the office and had grabbed the receiver. 'King here,' he barked into it.

'This is Sid Jones,' said a voice at the other end. 'I just couldn't make it last night, Mr. King; but look, I'll see you at my place tonight. I can't say any more. I'm being watched and I'm in danger, so — '

There was a click as the man hung up and the line went dead.

3

Ladies' Man

'I wish your people weren't so darned keen on pinching suspects,' Danny King said. 'I never had a chance to speak to the fellow when they nabbed him.'

The inspector stared at him in amazement and looked up at the clock over Danny's head. 'But they won't have got there yet,' he said. 'You were going to hold him on the phone until they got there.'

'If they haven't nabbed him, someone else has,' Danny said. 'He hung up on me.'

'The squad had instructions not to arrest until the man left the box,' the inspector said.

'Out of the blue, and back into it again just like that!' Danny groaned. 'This case gets screwier and screwier. We've got dames and thugs and guns already. All we want now is a nice juicy murder to round the job off.'

'You'll get that all right,' the inspector said gloomily. 'We've had two more hold-ups today, and a bad shooting affray in Soho.'

The telephone rang. 'Speaking,' the inspector said into the mouthpiece, and followed this with a few brief orders. 'The call-box was empty,' he told Danny. 'The squad car found it open and the man gone. So that's that.'

Danny went out.

In the street he pondered the problem facing him. He had to find the elusive Sid Jones in order to prevent the unloading of a vessel stacked with arms of all kinds. Only Sid Jones could tell him *when* and *where* the vessel was landing. Then he owed it to himself to discover the girl who had got him into the hands of the two thugs suspected of being concerned with the smuggling of arms. At any rate, he had a clue to the girl's identity. He hailed a taxi, giving the man the address of the jeweller in Bond Street who had been recommended by the expert.

'Yes, sir,' the jeweller said. 'I recall this watch very well. It's not a common make, and there aren't many like it in this country. Ah, yes! Here's our mark. Now all I have to do is to see if we have any name on our books against that number.'

He went off to find out. Danny leaned negligently upon the counter. When the jeweller came back, he had a book which he placed in front of Danny, pointing to a line on which was a number. Against the number was an address in Mayfair, and the name 'Mr. Karl Bronislawski'.

'Thank you,' Danny said, scribbling down the name and address.

Karl Bronislawski! So that would be the 'K' on the inscription. The next thing would be to get a look at Mr. Bronislawski, and then take a peep through the files in the records department. Danny got in his taxi and went off to Mayfair.

Mr. Bronislawski lived in a suite of modern flats in an old freestone mansion overlooking a small park. No one answered Danny's ring, and so he assumed the gentleman was out. He avoided ringing too much so as not to disturb the commissionaire, whom he had purposely avoided. Danny pulled a slender tool from his pocket and inserted it in the lock. There was a click and the door opened. Then, as he pushed the door to enter, he heard the lift whirr into activity. He had no time to get inside the small hall, and he stepped back into the passage.

The head and shoulders of a man appeared in the lift, and Danny gasped. The man in the lift was Sid Jones! His eyes were filled with a mixture of fear and pleading as, passing Danny, he laid a warning finger on his lips. But his eyes looked over Danny's shoulder and the lift went on upwards, gaining speed. Warned by the man's look, Danny said nothing, but he turned to face a dark, olive-skinned man who stood in the door of the apartment of Mr. Bronislawski.

'You rang, I think?' the man said in impeccable English. 'I was asleep. Won't you come in?'

'Thank you,' Danny said. 'I will.'

The apartment he entered was large

and magnificently furnished. His feet sank into thick rugs on the floor of a room which contained many works of art. Huge vases and great oil paintings were on display, while jade and ivory objects were scattered on small inlaid tables which were placed among the ornate furniture of the room. His host, who was dressed, but with a silk wrap over his shirt and trousers, waved Danny to a chair.

'And now,' he said, 'what can I do for you?' The menace in his tone was marked. His eyes were black and they glittered. He was as sleek and good-looking as a weasel is, and he looked as dangerous.

'You are Mr. Bronislawski?' Danny tried to make his voice sound as little like an accusation as possible.

The other nodded. 'And who have I the pleasure?' he said, lazily.

'Danny King,' Danny said slowly, 'of Scotland Yard.' The other looked up quickly at him, and his eyes glinted for a moment. His face hardened and then was serene again.

'Ah,' Mr. Bronislawski said, 'of Scotland Yard, eh? What brings you here, Mr.

King? Nothing serious, I hope. Of course, if I can help you in any way, I am yours to command. You are doubtless interested in my wish to become a naturalized British citizen, are you not?'

'As a matter of fact, I wasn't,' Danny said. 'But I shall be, Mr. Bronislawski.'

'Good,' said the other. 'It is a tedious business, this legal formality, is it not? And I'm sure that with your interest in my affairs, Mr. King, they will prosper.' His black eyes were full of mockery. 'But since you are not interested in these affairs just now, perhaps you will be so good as to tell me what it is that engages your attention.'

Danny took the watch from his pocket. As he did so, Bronislawski's hand flashed to a small table near at hand. An object fell to the floor and the hand came back bearing a silver casket.

'Cigarette, Mr. King?' his host enquired courteously, offering Danny the open casket.

Danny took one and produced his lighter. He placed the watch on the seat beside him, and as he drew back his arm from lighting his host's cigarette, his elbow knocked the watch, sending it spinning on to the carpet. Danny dived down to retrieve it, staring as he did so at the object Bronislawski had knocked off the table. But, quick as he was, his host was quicker. Like a serpent striking, the other man's hand closed over the watch.

He gave a smile at once courteous and deadly and turned the watch over in his hand. He spent a full minute examining the trinket; and then, looking up at Danny with his curious menacing air, said, 'Rather an uncommon make, is it not? Quite a charming thing for a woman, eh?' His tone was mocking. 'No doubt our friends in Bond Street have sent you to me as the purchaser of this pretty toy? They are right; I did buy it, but I can tell you nothing.' His mockery changed into a flat statement which was almost triumphant. 'The watch is not mine.'

'You hardly give me credit for brains, Mr. Bronislawski,' Danny said calmly. 'One does not expect a gentleman to wear a lady's wristlet watch. Obviously I have come to ask you who *is* the owner of this watch. Why beat about the bush?'

'I cannot tell you to whom this watch belongs because I do not know. I bought it, yes. But I gave it away.'

'Come now, Mr. Bronislawski,' Danny said. 'You buy an expensive watch. Then you, presumably, have it engraved, and yet you tell me that you don't know to whom it belongs!'

'My friend,' Bronislawski said, 'I do not know. There is, as you see, a lady in the case. There are times when the mind is a blank, when the memory is poor. Come, Mr. King, you are a man of the world. You know that one does not give a lady such a watch for feeding the pigeons in your charming Trafalgar Square, does one? Surely you do not wish to know the lady's name.'

'I must apologise for my ungallant curiosity in this matter,' Danny said, 'but I don't see why you should make such a mystery of it. I am a policeman. The niceties of your affairs with any lady or ladies do not interest me. What I want to know is who you gave this watch to. It may have been for feeding pigeons or for first prize in Sunday School for all I care. And, Mr. Bronislawski, you surely realize that this mysteriousness and this evasion are very bad tactics for a foreigner taking out naturalization papers.'

The undercurrent of Danny's speech was as chill and threatening as that of Bronislawski.

'You speak of mystery, Mr. King,' that gentleman replied. 'I don't like mysteries. I like to come to the point and to put all my cards on the table. There is, for instance, a mystery which annoys me very much — namely a door opened, I think, with a skeleton key. This is not a big mystery, perhaps — but perhaps also, those superiors of whom you speak will not like it either. After all, even a foreigner has his rights in this country, and your very excellent English law-courts are quick to see that those rights are upheld, are they not? This, I believe, is yours, Mr. King.' He handed Danny the slender piece of steel with which Danny had sprung his lock.

Danny King cursed himself again for his stupidity. Bronislawski had indeed called his bluff. No smile was on his face, but his glittering eyes plainly said, 'Laugh that one off.'

Danny cursed again.

'I see that we understand each other,' Danny said, 'and since that is so, perhaps we can leave the bush we have both been so carefully beating around and come out into the open. Since you won't tell me to whom you gave this watch, Mr. Bronislawski, perhaps you will be good enough to confirm that you did, in fact, give it to Sandra Mason.'

If Danny had hit Bronislawski full in the face he could not have produced a greater shock upon that gentleman. Bronislawski's jaw dropped, and he muttered some words in a foreign language. Danny picked up his ears at the sound of it.

'Yes, Mr. Bronislawski, you have been very foolish.' He bent down and picked up the photograph which Bronislawski had knocked off the table when he had reached for the casket. As he looked at the beautiful face of the girl he had met so strangely in the café, Danny began to

193

realize why he felt so savagely towards Bronislawski. 'An excellent likeness,' he remarked, 'but damned foolish of you to direct my attention to the fact that you wished to keep secret your association with the young lady.'

'Eh?' Bronislawski said. 'Aha, yes, quite!' He was smiling blandly again and seemed to have recovered himself. 'In spite of our differences, Mr. King, I find myself agreeing with you.'

Danny got up. He felt that Bronislawski had told him all he wanted to know. 'I suppose it's not much good asking you where I can find Miss Mason?' he inquired. But Bronislawski seemed not to have heard him, and only after some seconds did he reply.

'Oh! Ah yes, Miss Mason. A nice name, Mason, is it not? You English have such pleasant names. Mason,' he repeated, as if to himself. 'I think I shall take that name for my new English name. Oh, but of course, you wish to know where you can find the lady. I am afraid I'm not able to tell you. But should you care to drop in tonight at, say, nine o'clock, Miss Mason will be here. You can then ask her yourself.'

'O.K.,' Danny said, and went to the door. His host let him out into the hall, where Danny said, 'And I'd be less clumsy if I were you, the next time you have a visit from the Yard.'

Bronislawski's eyes glittered again. His face was a mask of hatred.

'Clumsiness is always foolish,' he said, 'and care of oneself could be advised in many quarters. *Au revoir*, Mr. King.' He closed the door blandly, leaving Danny guessing.

4

Beware of Bodies in Bedrooms

The door of Bronislawski's apartment closed behind Danny. The detective stood on the landing, looking up the lift shaft. But the lift was again below him and there was no sign of Sid Jones. Just then, Danny would have given a lot to know what that mystery man was doing in the place at all, but his presence there served to clinch Danny's conviction that somehow Jones, the girl Sandra Mason, and Bronislawski were all linked together. He had to discover the links and to trace the whole plot through them.

He went downstairs and found the commissionaire standing in a pool of sunlight. The man was surprised by Danny's sudden appearance.

'Tell me,' Danny said, 'does a Miss Mason live here?'

'Miss Mason, sir?' The commissionaire

was puzzled. 'I don't really know what — ' He saw Danny's card. 'Oh, of course, sir, you'll excuse me. I had no idea,' he went on. 'With the police, of course, it's different. No, sir, I don't know of any lady by that name. Would it be a young lady, sir?'

'Aged about twenty-three. About five foot two, with a mass of auburn hair and a fresh complexion,' Danny told him. 'She might be a fairly frequent visitor here. For instance — ' He dropped his voice. ' — she might have called occasionally on Mr. Bronislawski.'

The commissionaire permitted himself a grim little smile.

'A number do that, sir,' he said. 'Mr. Bronislawski is, ahem, popular with the ladies. But I don't know the names of the callers, sir. A lady such as you describe might very well be one, but I can't say her name is Mason. I don't know the name at all. There's a Miss Stammers.'

'And does she answer to this description?' Danny asked.

'Yes, sir,' was the answer. 'She calls fairly frequently on the gentleman you have mentioned. There's nothing wrong, sir, I hope?'

'Nothing,' Danny told him, explaining that Bronislawski was applying for naturalization and that he himself was checking up on information. He then bid the man good day and went back to the Yard.

★   ★   ★

'Have those two birds spilt any gaff yet?' he asked the inspector, only to be answered in the negative.

Danny then attended the identity parade, but failed to see Sandra Mason among the women assembled. He did not expect to find the object of his quest in Bronislawski's flat at nine that night either, and confided as much to his chief.

'I wish we could pull the blighter in,' he said. 'I'm damn sure he's mixed up in the whole business. Isn't there anything we can get him for? Surely, among all the red tape that immigrants are surrounded with, there's something that he's done or omitted to do. I don't mean we should hold him, but just get him out of the way so that we can go through his flat.'

'My dear Danny,' the chief said, 'after the way in which you delivered our visiting card this afternoon, I'm quite certain that we should find nothing. Why don't you go along to the records department and see if you can find a photograph of this gentleman in our files? We haven't anything under his name, of course.'

Danny did as he suggested and spent a profitless hour looking for Bronislawski's picture in the Rogues' Gallery. As he shut the last file with a frustrated snap, he said to the inspector in charge, 'I suppose there's nothing new?'

'Oh yes, there is,' the official said jovially. 'We've got one of the fellows in the Soho job. Identified by a bystander. The boys are on the way to pull him in. We've also got a new crop of wide boys. Why not have a look at them?'

Danny idly turned over the photographs the inspector handed him. One of them made him whistle with surprise. Looking up, he asked, 'Well, what do you know about him?'

The inspector glanced at the photo and searched among a pack of file cards.

'Sidney Mason — he's suspected, but never been arrested. Hasn't been seen lately. He's believed to have been killed in a train smash.'

'Not on your sweet life,' Danny said firmly. 'This bird is alive and kicking all right. In fact, this Sidney Mason is none other than that elusive man of mystery — the one and only Sid Jones. Say!' he exclaimed. 'Mason! Now we're getting somewhere.' He jumped off the table on which he had perched and picked up the file card and photo. 'Lend me these a tick,' he said. 'I've just got to show them to the chief.'

In his chief's office, he threw the documents down on the astonished official's desk and exclaimed,

'A clue at last! A very palpable clue!' He folded his arms and leaned against the wall proudly.

'What does this mean, King?' asked the chief. 'Who is this Mason, anyway?'

'Don't you see?' Danny said, jerking from the wall. 'It's Sid Jones, the mystery man. Sid Jones is Sidney Mason. And the girl's name is Mason. It's all beginning to fit together!'

'Humph!' The chief was impressed. 'We'd better get a check-up on this fellow,' he said. 'Of course, there may be no connection. You can't be sure that the girl gave you her right name, can you? She may have hit on 'Mason' out of the blue.'

'She may have done,' Danny said. 'But there's just one thing that makes it all Lombard Street to a China orange she didn't. When I told Bronislawski that the watch belonged to a girl called Mason, he acted as if he'd been thunderstruck. I'm darned sure that he didn't know the girl's name is Mason until I told him. She's been working under an alias as far as Bronislawski is concerned. Well, Miss Mason will have a lot of explaining to do when she meets Mr. Bronislawski.'

'I rather think that she will have to do more explaining than that,' the chief said. 'But see here, Danny, if you're going to contact this man Jones — or Mason, or whatever his real name is — you'd better get going.'

Danny looked at his watch and opened the office door. 'Well, so long,' he said. 'Keep your fingers crossed.'

He went out and passed through the corridor to his own office. On his desk was a letter with his name typewritten on it. There was no stamp, but the receiving clerk's time stamp showed the letter had been delivered by hand less than half an hour ago.

He picked it up and opened it. It was quite short and to the point. It was from Karl Bronislawski, regretting that he would be unable to keep his appointment for that evening, and giving an address in Maida Vale at which Danny could find Miss Sandra Mason. The note closed with a hope that the writer's flat would be safe from thieves and burglars during his brief absence.

Danny cursed himself again and put the note back on the table. He stood for some minutes with his hands in his pockets, and then put on his hat. A few minutes later, he was on the way to Maida Vale.

'Miss Mason's just gone out,' the

landlady told him at the address Bronis-lawski had given him. 'Miss Stammers is her stage name, you know. That's why I couldn't quite place her when you asked. Most of her gentlemen ask for Miss Stammers.'

Danny thanked her and went. His next move would he to Sid Jones' or Sid Mason's lodgings. These were in a small quiet street in East Ham, and Danny dismissed his taxi and took the tube. He sat in the noisy compartment as the train roared out of the bowels of London into the daylight of the industrial East End.

The lodgings of the man he wanted to see were not easy to find. Few people seemed to have heard of the road, but after a while Danny located the house, a dingy brick building in a small courtyard off an alley. The front door was open, and no one came to answer the bell which he could hear pealing away somewhere in the depths of the house. A smell of dampness, old cooking and cats assaulted him as he entered the hall. Some stairs led to the floor above. There was a stone-flagged passage running to the kitchen alongside the stairs, and two front rooms off the hall. The wallpaper was stained with damp. Danny noticed that the dark passage had only fittings for gas-light, and felt for his torch. A search revealed no sign of Mr. Jones, alias Mason, in any of the downstairs rooms and Danny began to ascend the stairs.

When he got to the top he found four doors led off the landing, one of which was open. The room inside was dark, the curtains closed. Danny entered and flashed his torch around. The beam swept over a chair, a washbasin on the floor, the iron headframe of a bed, and then the bent knees and dangling legs of a man lying across the mattress. There was no need for Danny to make a closer examination. The man was plainly dead. He came closer and flashed his torch on the pale face.

It was the mysterious Sid Jones. He lay on his back across the bed, blood from his back seeping into the sheets and mattress while a small blue hole in his chest showed where the bullet had entered. He was dressed simply in an open-neck shirt and trousers of some dark stuff. Around his waist, just peeping through the slit of the shirt, was a canvas body belt. The pale straw colour of the belt stood out from a mass of blue and red blotches of tattoo marks with which the man's chest and stomach were covered.

Danny put his hand on the dead man's body. The corpse was cold and had obviously been dead for some time. Furthermore, Danny's trained eyes could read signs that told him the unfortunate man had not met his death in that place, but had been carried there. He patted the trouser pockets but felt nothing in them except the outlines of some loose change and a cigarette-maker. He pulled up the shirt and saw that the body belt had a pouch, turned in so that the flap was next to the skin. Danny put his torch down and loosened the belt. When he had undone it so that he could open the flap, he felt inside the pouch and his fingers gripped a paper.

He drew it out and put it in his pocket, rearranging the flap and tightening the belt again. Hardly had he done this when he heard a noise behind him. Danny turned, but before he could make any real movement, a smashing blow crashed on his head and the room flashed full of glaring light as, with a dull roaring in his unconscious ears, he slumped to the floor.

5

Talk Fast, Lady!

Danny King blinked and saw a dim light from the darkened street stealing into the darker room. His mouth was dry and rough; his head ached, and sharp spasms of pain tore his skull apart each time he opened his eyes. He groaned aloud, running his hand through his hair. In this manner he found a bump on the back of his head as big as a pigeon's egg. He lay back against the bed's foot to recollect his bearings. As consciousness and memory came flooding back he struggled, groaning, to his feet. He looked down at the bed.

The body had disappeared! With an oath, he bent down and began to search in the dark for his torch. But he could not find it. He was still unsteady on his feet as he went down the stairs.

The house was as deserted as before. The alley was dark and cold in the moonless night. Danny walked out on to the main road and found a phone booth. Soon he was talking excitedly to the chief. By the time he had finished, he had decided what was to be done, and was ready to put his plan into action. Just as he replaced the phone and turned to open the kiosk door, the headlight of a passing car illuminated a girl passing by. Danny stiffened. The girl was Sandra Mason. He left the kiosk and followed.

Sandra Mason walked on until she came to the alleyway in which Sid Jones' lodgings were situated. Certain now of where the girl was going, Danny hung back to let the girl get ahead. When he did arrive at the house door, the girl was nowhere to be seen; but he heard her moving about upstairs, and could see the flash of a torch being swung around as if the girl was looking for something. Soundlessly, Danny crept up the stairs and peered into the room in which Sid Jones' body had been. The girl knelt on the floor facing the bed, turning over a heap of papers which were lighted by the beam of the torch beside her.

'Excuse me,' Danny said softly.

The girl sprang up with a startled cry, picking up the torch and shining it full into Danny's face.

'Oh,' she said. 'So it's you.'

'Yes,' Danny said, 'it's me. If I were you, I'd come quietly. I've several things I want to discuss with you.'

'Oh, I — oh, all right,' Sandra Mason said nervously. 'But let's get out of this room, for heaven's sake.'

'This room will do admirably, I think,' Danny said, 'There's a gas-light on the wall, if you'll be so good as to find it with the torch.'

When the gas had been lighted, Danny was able to see the girl properly for the first time since he had met her in the café. She was white and drawn. 'Sit down,' he ordered, indicating the bed. The girl looked first at the bed and then at Danny. Then she sat, very gingerly, on the bed's extreme edge.

'Now,' Danny said, 'perhaps you'll explain.'

'Explain what?' Sandra Mason demanded.

'Well, you might begin by explaining

first of all how it is that a perfectly innocent young man like myself comes to be set on by a couple of tough eggs merely because he is escorting you through the West End. And you could end by explaining what you are doing here.'

'I warned you that two men were after me,' Sandra said. 'Anyway,' she went on, 'who are you to ask questions?'

'I'm just a plain ordinary copper,' Danny told her, 'but I'm very, very interested in knowing what you are doing in all this.'

The girl looked at him in amazement. 'A copper?' she said. 'But I don't understand. What are you doing here?'

'I came here to meet a friend of mine,' Danny replied. 'A namesake of yours — Mr. Sidney Mason.'

If he had struck her, he could not have shocked the girl more profoundly. He went over to her and took the torch out of her hand.

'This is mine, I believe,' he said. 'I'll have it back now. And now, Miss Mason, will you explain how you not only get me a crack over the head by two hired thugs, but why you also set on me yourself, and incidentally did the job of knocking me unconscious far more efficiently than they did?'

Sandra sat on the bed, the picture of misery. Her self-confident air had now gone. Danny could see she was all in. She looked up at him.

'I suppose,' she said, 'I'm under arrest. I suppose anything I say will be used in evidence against me? Is that it?'

'I ought to warn you,' Danny said. 'But somehow I feel that you won't be locked up yet. The best thing you can do is to come clean and tell me the whole story. Mind you, I know certain parts of it here and there. So don't make the mistake of trying to invent things. Talk fast, lady, and talk true.'

'I suppose I might as well,' Sandra said in a hollow, miserable voice. 'I suppose you'll want to know what I'm doing here. Well, I came to find my brother. This used to be his room.'

'And you found me here instead, and tapped me on the head for old times' sake?' Danny said.

The girl shook her head. 'No,' she said. 'Someone else did that. Somebody got here before me. When I arrived, you were lying on the floor, I suppose, and — ' She broke off. 'Oh! I can't stand it! It was all so horrible. Poor Sid!'

Danny lit a cigarette and gave it to the girl. He said gently, 'You found your brother had been killed, didn't you? The thing which you had feared had happened. That was it, wasn't it?'

The girl looked at him in wonder. Her lovely face was ashen with grief. 'You seem to know everything about it,' she said dully. Then fire came into her tone. 'Why did you kill my brother?'

This time Danny was amazed. 'But I didn't kill him,' he said. 'Like you, I came here and found him. He was already dead when I arrived.'

Sandra looked at him quickly, but Danny gave her no opportunity to speak. He went on, 'And what I would very much like to know is — where's the body now?'

Sandra seemed to be in a daze. She said in a small, strangled voice, 'If you didn't kill Sidney, then who did?'

'Now, see here,' Danny said. 'These questions and counter-questions have been getting us nowhere. I'm the policeman and you're the suspect. Suppose you answer me while I ask you a few plain simple questions. We can both learn a lot then.'

Sandra gulped. 'Go on,' she said. 'I'll try to answer.'

'In the first place,' Danny said, 'did you or did you not know that I had an appointment to meet your brother when you spoke to me in the café?'

The wonder on the girl's face told Danny his answer before she spoke. 'No, truly I didn't,' she said. 'I didn't know you were a detective, either. I knew Sidney was going to the café. And I knew that he was in danger. You see, Sidney got mixed up with some business to do with smuggling guns. Those two men, Nobby and the other one, were in it too. I didn't like it, and I begged Sid to give the whole thing up and get an honest job. Well, I gave him some money, and then he promised me he'd break away from the gang. But he didn't, and I kept on and on at him until he began to realise he was doing wrong, and at last he agreed to tell everything to the police. Later, he told me the gang would never let him out of their sight because he had something they wanted. So that night I went down to the café where we usually went at night, and I saw two thugs waiting about. Then it suddenly occurred to me that if I could behave as though Sid was in the offing, I had every chance of drawing them away from Sid and giving him a chance to get away. When I saw you sitting at Sid's table in the corner alone, I thought you might be able to help me. You looked so strong and dependable.'

'Thanks.'

'You see,' went on Sandra, 'I thought if I could get you to walk out of the place with me, those two would follow us. In the dim light you vaguely looked like Sid, and I thought there was a remote chance they would mistake you for him.'

Danny rubbed his much-bruised head. 'Your hunch was right,' he said ruefully. 'Now, tell me something else: who's this man they call Juke?'

'Juke?' Sandra queried. 'Oh, you mean the Duke. That's what they called Sid. He lodged with me for a time, and the gang used to ring up and ask for the Duke.'

'That was about the time you met Bronislawski, wasn't it?' Danny said.

Sandra sighed. 'So you know about Karl too!'

'I know a little about Karl, and I'd like to know a lot more,' Danny said. 'For instance, why did you tell him your name was Stammers?'

'Because — oh, it's silly, I suppose, to you — but it was an idea of Sid's. He said because of what he was doing and one thing and another, it would be best if we both split up and lived separately. He wanted to change his name, and he said I ought to change mine too. Why he chose Jones for himself and Stammers for me, I don't know.'

'Where did you meet Bronislawski?'

'At a night club. I was a dancer there.'

'I see,' Danny said. 'Well, Miss Mason, there's just one thing I don't understand. If your brother was leaving, and if those two thugs were after him, how on earth did you come into the picture? I mean, did you know he was being followed, or did you expect to find him in the café? And in any case, if these fellows knew him, how did you expect them to mistake me for him?'

'Well, you see, Sid had said he was giving up the gang so many times that I never believed him when he promised. I went round to his digs the afternoon I met you and I found a note he had written arranging to meet someone — it didn't say who — in the café at eleven o'clock that night. I guessed he was up to no good. So I hung around until he came back, and he told me that he had to meet someone connected with the police, and that he was really going to come clean. He was also a bit scared that the gang would get nasty. After he'd gone, I could see the risk Sid was taking, so I decided to go to the meeting place in case Sid got into trouble and needed a hand.'

'You've got guts,' Danny said admiringly.

Sandra was in no mood for compliments. 'Well, Sid didn't turn up. I waited

216

for quite a while, then I saw you come in.'

'Wait a minute,' Danny broke in. 'Didn't it occur to you that I was the man Sid was going to meet?'

The girl smiled wanly. Danny decided that, even with her make-up ruined by tears, she was still the prettiest girl he had ever seen when she smiled.

'No, it didn't.'

'Miss Mason,' Danny said, 'there's just one more question I want to ask you. At least, it's two really, but it all leads to the same thing. The question is this: who do you think killed your brother, and where is your brother now?'

Sandra Mason did not answer at once. Then she spoke in a rush. 'Oh, it's surely obvious who killed him,' she said. 'Of course it's this gang. Nobby and his friend, most likely. But I can tell you the other answer. I've got Sid. I — I took his body home — to my place in Maida Vale!'

6

Fight for Your Love!

The girl's statement shook Danny. 'You mean you actually *moved* the body?'

Sandra nodded. 'Yes, you see — '

'Then it *was* you who hit me on the head!' Danny accused.

Sandra Mason looked apologetic. 'Not exactly,' she explained. 'You see, we didn't know — '

'Who's *we*?' Danny exclaimed. 'I was going to point out that you could hardly have carried the body yourself. Who was the other?'

'Oh, it was Karl who knocked you out. But he didn't know you were a police-officer, and he wouldn't let me into the room, so I couldn't see you.'

'So you think Karl didn't know me, eh?'

'No, why should he? Did you know him?'

'Now, look here, young lady,' Danny said, 'let's stop this question-and-answer business and get down to a little serious information. I'll do the asking; you just tell me what you know, and we'll get along fine. You're in a tough spot, you know, and a little cooperation on your part will help things a lot. Now, tell me why you came here.'

Sandra Mason looked at him with a resigned air. She had opened her mouth to object to Danny's dictating, but his concluding words prevented her outburst. Instead, she gave a little shrug, and said, 'Well, you see, I'd been talking to Karl about Sid, and how I wanted Sid to turn honest. So Karl suggested that we should go down and get Sid to come with us and give himself up while we could keep an eye on him. We came on down here, and that's how — ' She paused and bit her lip, then went on. 'It was then I found that Sid had been killed.'

'Did you find him, or did Bronislaw-ski?'

'Karl did,' the girl said. Her face again assumed the strained look. 'You see, if I had gone up, Sid would only have argued. So Karl went. The idea was that he should tell Sid I was ill and that he'd been sent to fetch me.'

'And how long was Bronislawski away from you when he went up to your brother?'

'About ten minutes, I think.' The girl stiffened. 'Why? Are you suggesting that Karl killed my brother?'

'I'm not suggesting anything,' Danny snapped at her. 'I'm just asking questions. Remember? Go on answering.'

The girl's eyes flashed rebellion, but she did no more than shrug as she continued, 'Well, we had a taxi in the main road and I waited there. Karl came back and explained to me what had happened. I — I was so shocked and upset that I couldn't believe it. So then, after a time, we went back to get him — to get Sid's body, I mean — and that was where we found you here.'

Danny grunted. 'I suppose your friend Bronislawski simply came out carrying Sid and said, 'There's another guy in there, but I slugged him'; and you said,

'Oh, that's all right', and you both beat it?'

Sandra was silent for a minute. Then, in a small voice: 'I know it sounds funny, but in fact that's almost what we did say.'

Danny snorted. 'It sounds so far-fetched,' he said, 'that even if I wanted to believe it, I couldn't. You can't get out of it like that, Miss Mason. You're in a spot, and even if I did believe you, you're still in a spot.' He rounded on her fiercely. 'Why exactly did you take your brother's body back to Maida Vale? Don't tell me it was because you wanted it for a keepsake.'

As soon as the words were out of his mouth, Danny regretted them.

Sandra Mason sprang up, her eyes flashing; her hand darted out, catching Danny a stinging smack on the cheek.

'You beast,' the girl cried. 'You cynical beast!' She stood in front of him as he retreated, her eyes flashing.

'All right, all right,' Danny said. 'Relax, will you? I'm sorry for the crack. Now, why not come clean and tell me the truth? You took your brother's body because he had something you wanted. It wasn't in his pockets, and so you took the body. Now, what was it?'

'Find out yourself, you slick copper,' Sandra yelled angrily.

'All right, then,' Danny said. 'If you won't tell me, I'll tell you. Sidney Mason had information about the landing of arms into this country. He had the name of the ship, the day and the hour and the place at which she was docking. And he carried this information on his skin. You thought it was tattooed on him.' Danny's voice dropped. 'Now, I'll tell you something you don't know. Your brother wasn't a crook.' At his words she raised her head and looked full at him. 'He was a special agent working for Scotland Yard,' Danny explained. 'He was engaged in tracking down an organization which is at work forming the underworld of London and the other great cities of England into one big gang. His part was to prevent them from obtaining these arms. He got the information about the ship, and was to give it to me. Then you chipped in. How you found out he had this information, I don't know, but that is what you were after. When you got him back to Maida Vale, you couldn't find it. So you came back here to look for it.'

'You're right,' Sandra in a low voice. 'He did tell me about it. He said if ever anything happened to him I was to send the information to Scotland Yard. He told me nothing else, I swear. He didn't even tell me what it was. All he said was that it was something about the gang, and that I should recognize it because it was the name of a ship, a place and a date, and he said he kept it on his skin.'

Danny nodded. 'I suppose, when you and Bronislawski came here to get the body, you thought I was one of the gang.'

'Yes,' Sandra said. 'You see, I told Karl about this information which Sid had, and he suggested we should take him to my place. We didn't know who would come, you see, and we thought it would be safer there. Karl told me to wait downstairs and went up. He dragged Sid's body down the stairs, and when he got to the bottom, he told me about you and how he had knocked you out. But he didn't say who you were. The taxi driver thought Sid was drunk.'

'Karl knew me all right,' Danny said. 'I was talking to your friend Karl only this afternoon.'

'But I didn't know you knew him.'

'I didn't, until *you* introduced us.'

'*I* introduced you? But I don't understand.'

'You had a watch,' Danny told her. 'Remember? You see, as a policeman, it's part of my job to be curious about watches, especially engraved watches.'

'But surely,' Sandra said, 'if Karl knew you, why did he hit you?'

'Now then, there you go again,' Danny warned her, 'asking questions. Tell me one thing and then I'm through. Was there a belt around your brother's body when you first saw him — I mean, when Karl had brought him downstairs? Think hard and try to remember — because this is the most important thing of all.'

Sandra puckered her face in an effort to remember. Then she said, 'No, I'm certain there wasn't because, when we got back, Karl undressed Sid and there was nothing. Not even a paper in his pocket.

We couldn't find any tattoo mark on his body that told us what we needed to know.'

'What did you do then?'

'Well, Karl said I should go to bed, and I agreed. But when he'd gone I took a taxi and came back here. Then you came in, and that's all I know — '

Sandra spun round as heavy footsteps sounded behind her.

'That was very foolish of you, my dear, because now I shall probably have to kill you as well as Mr. King,' said a voice from the door.

Danny whirled round to see the evil face of Bronislawski, who was standing in the door, holding a pistol with an unusually long barrel. Bronislawski moved forward.

'You have a paper in your pocket, King. Give it to me.'

His eyes glittered evilly; the pistol in his hand was steady as a rock.

Danny made no move.

'Give it to me,' Bronislawski said, 'and don't get any funny ideas. I warned you to be careful, and you were so sure you could be smart, weren't you?'

'I don't know what you're talking about, Bronislawski,' Danny said. 'Perhaps if you will explain yourself, we can get along a lot better.'

'Very well, then,' Bronislawski said. 'I will make myself plain. Miss Mason, there is a small piece of paper in Mr. King's pocket. Get it.'

Under the threat of the pistol, Sandra moved across to Danny and began to go through his pockets. Even under the circumstances, the nearness of the girl filled Danny with strange feelings. He could hardly restrain the impulse to take her in his arms. Bronislawski, who was watching the pair of them like a hawk, misinterpreted his thoughts.

'I wouldn't do that if I were you, Mr. King,' he said. 'Although Miss Mason's charming and shapely body is in front of yours, I hardly think it is tough enough to stop a bullet at this range. I should be sorry to shoot you, my dear,' he went on, addressing himself to Sandra, 'while your back is still turned. When I kill you, I want to see you as you feel the bullets . . . So, you were merely interested in the unfortunate Sid Jones because he was the boyfriend of your great pal, were you? And you didn't think that, even as you told me your lies, I knew he was your brother and that your name, like his, was Mason — ' He broke off as Sandra pulled from Danny's pocket a crumpled piece of soiled notepaper. Bronislawski came forward and seized it from the girl's fingers.

'Right,' he said. 'Now stand over there by him. Don't either of you move a finger. Keep your hands up, King, and both of you keep your backs to the wall.'

His evil eyes never left their faces as he pushed the paper into his breast pocket, covering them with his gun. Danny went back slowly against the wall. As he did so, his hand touched lightly against something hot. The globe of the gas-light! In a flash he struck the heated glass globe with his clenched fist, smashing it to the floor and extinguishing the light. With his other hand he sent Sandra Mason staggering away from him to the floor as he himself crashed to the ground.

Bronislawski's pistol exploded with a strangled noise like a paper bag going off, and then Danny had him by the legs. With a heave he threw the man off his balance and heard the heavy gun clatter to the ground. He aimed twice with his fist at where he imagined Bronislawski's head would be, but he hit nothing.

Then a sickening blow struck him in the face, and before he could recover, Bronislawski was on top of him and two strong hands gripped his throat. At once he raised his knees and hit something soft. He heard a groan and the grip relaxed. Rising to his feet he milled around in the dark, searching for his enemy. He could hear Sandra groaning and then heard Bronislawski behind him. Quick as a flash he turned and struck: his fist, not quite clenched, flailed in the air, and his fingers hooked into cloth. There was a ripping, tearing sound, and then two hands grappled him. Kicking and cursing, Bronislawski clawed at him. Danny began to punch at his enemy's body. He got two good blows home when his foot struck the pistol. It slithered along the floor. Bronislawski heard it too, but before he could break away from

Danny's clinch, Sandra called, 'I've got it! I've got the gun! Where is he, Danny?'

Bronislawski began to buck like a colt to extricate himself from Danny's grasp, and then the pistol exploded again. A great light broke in front of Danny's eyes and he felt as if a piece of ice had been drawn over his skull. Then everything went black and he passed out.

7

The Brute

When Danny came to, he was conscious of the fact that he was lying in bed, that everything around him was white, and that he felt sick and had a splitting headache. He groaned as he opened his eyes to see a nurse standing by his bed. Then he struggled to get up.

'You must lie down and rest,' the nurse said. 'You're not allowed to talk.' Strangely enough, Danny found himself relieved at her words, and a great peace enveloped him as he slipped into sleep again.

He awoke to find the chief at his bedside. The pain in his head was now a hazy ache. He still felt sick.

'Well, Danny,' the chief said, 'you've a lot to be thankful for, and that thick skull of yours is one of those things.'

'What happened?' Danny said. 'Where's Miss Mason?'

The chief shook his head. 'We were hoping you could tell us that,' he said. 'But what was Miss Mason doing? How did she come into it?'

'She was with me,' Danny said. 'I was struggling with Bronislawski and she had the gun.'

He began to tell the chief of the happenings in Sid Mason's lodgings. When he had finished, the chief said, 'All this was last night. You've been unconscious twenty-four hours. We've been waiting for you to come round. You were found by the squad when they got there after your phone call. They found you lying on the floor with a furrow in your skull as if it had been ploughed. You're damn lucky to be alive.'

'I only wish to heaven I'd taken a look at that damn paper,' Danny said. 'Bronislawski has it now. But can't you find him and bring him in, Chief?'

'We're looking for him now,' the chief said. 'We've got a manhunt on like nobody's business. By the way, we raided the Mason girl's lodgings. We found Mason's body there — and also a photo of Bronislawski, alias Petroff, who used to hang out down Wapping in the old days. Yes, we checked the picture against the records, and it's Petroff all right. We've had a warrant out for him for years for another job he did. But there's been no sign of the Mason girl, and I think she's gone to ground with him . . . Well, it's only a matter of time. They can't escape the dragnet we've got out.'

'But she's not in with him,' Danny protested. 'You're more likely to drag her out of the river.'

The chief shook his head and laughed. 'You'd better get plenty of rest,' he said. 'You're badly knocked up. When you're fit to report back, we'll have both these birds laid by the heels.'

Left to himself, Danny lay back on his pillow, his mind a whirl of thoughts. Somewhere out there in London was Sandra, with a man who was little better than a killer. Danny began to recall the facts of the Petroff case. Petroff was a criminal whose activities ranged from warehouse robberies to running dope-dives. There had been some ugly rumours about his connection with some horribly mutilated corpses of women which had been dragged from the river, although the coroner found that the gashes and weals were the result of ships' propellers. But that was the kind of reputation Petroff had — nasty.

Danny asked himself why he should care about Sandra Mason's fate, but all he could arrive at was the fact that he *did* care, and cared very much. He had been on the Petroff job and he was the detective who had discovered the gang's hideout. He felt caged and helpless lying there in bed when all his instincts urged him to be up and searching for Sandra and the man she knew as Bronislawski.

The day faded to dusk. The nurse came and went, and at last the hospital was still and silent. Danny crept uncertainly from the bed and opened the steel locker by the washstand. He sighed with relief as he realized that they had not taken away his clothes. When he had finished dressing, he opened the window and crept onto the fire escape. It was the work of a few moments to descend and to gain the street. Then he felt in his pockets. His wallet and money were still there. Only his pistol and torch were missing. He hailed a passing taxi and gave an address in East London. From there he made his way on foot to the old tumbledown house by the river which had always been the hideout of the Petroff gang. Underworld gossip held that the gang still met in an old cellar.

Stealing quietly among the shattered walls and arches, Danny approached the burnt-out shell of the warehouse. The four walls, roofless and shattered, remained standing in jagged clumps of brick and stonework, but of any entrance to the alleged crypt there was no sign. Tiptoeing round the burned walls, Danny stepped on something soft. He thought at first it was some paper or mud, but a metallic crunch as his weight came down on it made him bend and pick it up.

In the dim light he could just see it was a purse such as might have come from a woman's handbag. He opened it and found inside a few coppers and some silver. But about the purse hung the scent of a perfume which Danny knew at once. It was Sandra's. His thoughts raced and his fists clenched. So she was somewhere near here!

He sat down in the shadow of the wall to try to recollect the place as it had been when the gang had made use of the warehouse. He remembered that there had been, in the warehouse floor, a steel cover. He knew that he had no chance of finding the cover at all on such a dark night, and with all the rubble and filth which covered the ground. He got up and walked towards the river.

A narrow causeway separated the burnt-out buildings from the waterfront. The water level here was some ten feet below the road. Suddenly Danny froze. A man came from behind a wall a few yards away and went towards the river. He was outlined against the lighter surface of the water for an instant, and then disappeared downwards in a series of jerks. Danny realized that there would be some steps down which the man had gone, when he suddenly heard footsteps below him. Then there came a grating noise and a light faintly shone across the water.

So that was it! There was an entrance to the crypt right below him. He ran to the steps and looked down. He could see a narrow ledge some two feet above water level, just wide enough for a man to stand on. The tide was out, and a line of weed showed that when the tide came in, the ledge would be covered. Danny crept along the ledge, feeling the wall for a door.

He found the door some twenty feet along from the steps. His fingers told him it was a steel door and that it was open. He inched it wide enough for him to squeeze through. In front of him was a wall with steps running off right and left. Down one of these steps the light shone faintly. The other stairway was dark.

'Go down and shut the door,' he heard a voice say. 'The tide'll turn in an hour or so, and we don't want the water in.'

There was a muttered reply, and then boots clattered on the steps above him. He ascended the other darkened flight as the footsteps came down, and with his heart pounding his ribs he saw the man close the door and go back up the stairs. Danny stood where he was, undecided as to what to do.

Behind him, he could feel another door at the top of the steps, and this he opened.

He found himself looking down into a long room with a vaulted roof and a stone-flagged floor. He was standing on a landing from which steps led down to the room below. An electric fire was burning in one corner, illuminating the room with a faint light. In the opposite corner of the room was a camp bed on which was a pile of rugs or blankets.

Danny lay full-length on the stone floor of the landing and studied the scene below. He could see a door which led into another part of the crypt, and even as he noticed it, the door opened and a light flashed on. Danny froze in his place, for the man who entered was none other than Petroff, alias Bronislawski. He carried a small cane in his hand, went to the bed, and struck the heap of rugs a blow which cracked like a revolver shot. There was a cry of pain and a flurry of blankets, and a girl in evening dress sprang from the bed.

It was Sandra!

Bronislawski raised the cane and struck her again and again as she ducked and swerved to avoid him. At last, he stepped on the rug and struck savagely at the girl to drive her back. Sandra tried to avoid the blows which the man showered on her. But though she made no sound as each blow raised a red welt on her body's whiteness, the savage attack was too much for her, and she swayed as though she were about to faint. Bronislawski threw his cane into the corner. Then he went to the door and called. A man came in with a bowl of water, which he poured over Sandra at Bronislawski's instructions.

'Cripes, boss, you'll do for this judy,' the man said. He was a hulking specimen with a bestial nature written all over his face.

'That is none of your business,' Bronislawski said, 'and it is time that you and Paul were on your way. Now remember, the police are looking for me, so be careful. Whatever happens, no one must know where I am until the ship docks. If the others ask you where I am, you don't know. Understand?'

'O.K., boss,' the man said, and went out.

Bronislawski went to a cupboard and poured himself a drink. Danny King, lying hidden above him, could hear two men going down the other stairs and out through the door to the steps that led to the street.

The sound elated him. He did not know whether there would be any others left in the other part of the crypt, but at least there were two he did not have to reckon with. A groan made him direct his attention to Sandra, who was now lying face-downwards on the floor. The girl struggled to sit up.

Bronislawski moved across to her. 'So you have decided to take an interest in things?' he said.

'You *beast!*' the girl said. 'You *foul beast!*'

'Some men,' he said, 'would not be so patient as I. Oh, I'm not going to hurt

239

you again! I ought to kill you, but I know a better way to punish you. You are going to ask me to give you my kisses; you are going to go down on your knees and beg for them.'

He was on his feet, towering over the girl; his hands grabbed her by her shoulders as he forced her backwards. But Sandra leaped to her feet and ran from him towards the steps at the top of which Danny was lying. The detective had stood as much as he could of the scene below, and even as the girl moved, he was about to attempt a bluff that would stop Bronislawski. He stood up, and as he did so, Bronislawski, moving after the girl, passed under the wall by the steps. Danny dropped down upon him, striking the man with his knees and bearing him to the floor.

'*Danny!*' Sandra cried out, but the young man had no time to answer her. The man below him was fighting like a tiger, and as the detective struggled to secure a lock which would pin his opponent to the ground, the gangster threw him off his body with an expert heave which told Danny that he would need all his wrestling skill to win. Bronislawski leaped to his feet and ran to the cupboard from which he had taken the bottle. He reached it a good yard in front of Danny, and his hand came out of the cupboard with a gun.

Flame stabbed from the Luger's muzzle and the shot crashed out, whirring and splatting as it ricocheted around the stone-flagged vault. Then Danny closed with his enemy. His two hands were round the gun, forcing it down between his legs until he was able to grip it between his knees.

For a second he and Bronislawski stayed like this, glaring hate into each other's eyes while they fought with their free hands for a hold. Then Danny released the gangster's hand, and as the latter struggled to bring the gun up, Danny's fist struck him full on the jaw and he toppled back, the gun falling to the ground with a clatter. Before the other man could recover, Danny seized the weapon and turned to his enemy who was just rising from the floor.

'Get 'em up, Petroff,' Danny gritted out, a glow of triumph on his face.

Something struck his knee and fell with a clatter to the floor. It was the magazine of the gun, which had jerked loose in the struggle. The gangster, who had been leaning against the cupboard, sprang in, swinging the whisky bottle at Danny's head. The bottle flew from his hand as he missed Danny and struck Sandra, who was closing in on the two struggling men, full on the chest and sent her to the floor. Danny ducked under the man's guard and hit him again on the chin and once to the body. But the man still came on. His knee jerked up, striking Danny in the stomach.

A wave of agony spread over the detective and he crumpled up, sliding to the floor. Bronislawski caught up a chair and swung it down on his helpless opponent. If the blow had landed, it would have knocked Danny down for keeps; but as the chair swung down, the whisky bottle, thrown by Sandra, clattered against the chair and broke, sending the liquor into Bronislawski's eyes. The man screamed and staggered back while Danny rose from the floor and grappled with him. Bronislawski's hands were up at his face, and as Danny blundered towards him, the gangster did nothing but rub into his blinded eyes. Sick with pain and dizziness, Danny measured his punch and smashed a right to Bronislawski's jaw. The gangster went down as if he'd been poleaxed.

Sandra handed the gun to Danny. He shook his head wearily, leaning against the wall of the vault. 'We've got to get out of here.'

The girl nodded. Meanwhile, Danny tore the rug to strips and began to bind the prostrate gangster. He was thus engaged when the door at the top of the steps opened and a man came in.

'Hey!' the man shouted as soon as he saw what was going on. He came running toward Danny, a gun in his hand. 'C'mon,' the newcomer said. 'Get them up and stand over there. You too!' he gritted at the girl.

Danny stood against the wall.

'Hey Paul!' the man called, and at his

shout, another man came into the vault, cursing as his eyes took in the scene below. This second man cut the bindings away from Bronislawski, and after a few minutes succeeded in bringing him round.

'It's time we were flitting, boss,' the man called Paul said. 'The ship's been sighted and the lorries are on the way to meet her.'

Bronislawski stood up. His eyes glittered with hate as he looked at Danny and Sandra. 'Tie them up,' he said. 'We shan't want them anymore. We shan't want this place either. Tie them up and pull the plug out, and let them drown when the tide comes in.'

He stood over his two prostrate victims. His grinning face gloated down at Danny as he said, 'I thought I'd seen the last of you, copper, when I left Mason's place. But the girl missed you when she let drive with the gun. If it had been me, I'd not have missed, but I didn't have time to wait to find out if you'd been killed. This time, I'm going to make sure. This vault, as perhaps you've noticed, is on the waterfront, and all of it except three feet is below water level at high tide. This place has been useful to me in the past, and I hate to leave it. However, if it can take care of a pair of troublemakers like yourself and Miss Mason, it'll still be doing a useful job for me. In about two hours you will be drowned like rats.'

He turned on his heel and went up the steps, followed by the two thugs who had been engaged in binding Danny and Sandra while he addressed them. The policeman and the girl heard him in hopeless silence, bound and gagged like two trussed chickens. At the top of the steps he turned and called, 'For you, it is farewell forever.'

He went out through the door, which clanged behind him. Danny heard a confused scraping noise and then a dark, noisome draught of air blew over him. He looked to the wall and saw that a large stone had been removed and that water was flowing through the hole. It came into the vault in a steady flood from the river and spread across the floor. Fascinated, he watched it forming pools and running along the cracks between the flags.

No sound could be heard in the vault except the stertorious breathing of the captives and the lapping of the water. Bronislawski's intentions were only too plain. He had locked the vault and had removed one of the stones in the wall between the vault and the river, allowing the water to enter. It would rise with the tide until it was a full six feet deep. And Danny and Sandra, lying helpless on the floor, would be at the bottom of the silent waters until the tide receded.

8

Trapped!

His hands were tied behind his back, his feet were bent upwards and lashed to his hands, his mouth was gagged tightly. Danny was in a desperate situation as the water flowed towards him. A few feet of it would suffice to cover him and Sandra. Then, as Danny watched the dirty-brown river water reaching out fingers to him, he noticed also the jagged, broken glass of the whisky bottle. By hunching his shoulders and rolling his body, he began to struggle towards the glass.

It was slow and painful work, and when he had reached it he had to undergo the painful gymnastics of turning completely over to get the glass at the rope which bound him. Even then it seemed a forlorn hope, because though his fingers could feel the smooth surface of the bottle, he found that each time he attempted to rub the rope against the edge, the bottle slipped away and he had to move painfully back towards it.

But luck favoured Danny. The floor of the vault was rough and the flags which paved it were uneven. The bottle, moving backwards, lodged against a crevice in the floor and canted upwards at an angle. Watched by Sandra's anxious eyes, Danny put the rope that joined his feet and hands against the broken bottle.

The water came steadily into the vault and lapped around him, as he rocked and swayed in his desperate effort to free himself and the girl who lay bound with him.

Strand after strand of the rope parted, and still he was a prisoner. The water was coming in faster. Already it was a couple of inches deep and Sandra Mason's hair floated up from her prostrate head like seaweed. At last, after much painful sawing, the last strand parted and Danny was able to stretch himself out full-length. For two seconds he lay still, luxuriating in the release of his limbs. Then he sat up and began to saw away at the rope which bound his hands behind him. The jagged glass cut his fingers and wrists. His efforts tired him considerably and several times he had to stop to rest.

The water was now rising rapidly, and as the tide mounted higher and higher in the river outside, the water surged in and withdrew, and Danny's sawing raised eddies so that Sandra's face was often half-covered with water. His eyes were frantic above the gag that bound her lips. She tried to keep her head above the water, but the strain on her muscles was so great that she was forced to let her head relax into it. The surge and eddy of the flood lapped her face and filled her mouth as she gasped for breath. Her plight made Danny saw at his bonds even more desperately. He could feel the glass biting into the rope, and though his bound arms ached and every muscle of his body cried out in protest against the labour, he carried grimly on.

At last his hands were free! The last strand of rope fell away. Danny staggered up on his numbed hands, dragged his feet over to where Sandra was lying, and raised her from the floor into his arms.

The water was now so deep that if he had been only a minute later the girl would have been drowned. Holding her head against his knees, Danny tore Sandra's gag off and then his own. The girl's eyes were full of gratitude. Danny kissed her in utter relief. For a second their lips clung together, and then Sandra said with a smile:

'Don't you think you ought to try to free my hands?'

Danny nodded and pulled her over to the wall so that, leaning against it, she could keep above the rising water. He gingerly raised himself up and searched in the cupboard from which Bronislawski had produced the bottle of whisky. With a cry of triumph, he produced a knife, and in a few minutes he had completely freed the girl and himself.

'And now to get out,' he said.

But the words were not equal to the deed. One by one he examined the doors and found them locked. There was no way out. The water by this time was knee-high.

'I didn't scream when that brute beat me,' Sandra said breathlessly. 'I wasn't going to give him the satisfaction of letting him see I was scared.' She glanced round her hopelessly. 'Well, Danny, what do we do now?'

'We'll find some way of getting out,' he replied with a certainty he was far from feeling.

Sandra put her hand on his shoulder.

'Look, Danny,' she said, 'you can't kid me. I'm not a little girl, you know. I know that we're for it and that we probably shan't get out of here alive. But tell me just one thing. Why did you kiss me just now?' She looked steadily into his eyes so that Danny became almost embarrassed.

'Heck!' he said. 'If that isn't just like a woman. Here we are in a jam that's as bad as any I've ever been in, just about to be drowned like rats in a trap, and you ask a fool question like that!'

'It may be a fool question, Danny,' Sandra said, 'but it's important. It's always important to a woman, and to me it's very important.'

Something in her voice made Danny pause and look at her. He pulled her to him and kissed her again.

'I love you, I guess,' he muttered. 'But a fat lot of good that's going to do us now.'

'What's that up there?' Sandra said, pointing.

Danny looked upwards hopefully. His face brightened. 'Seems like a trapdoor leading to the warehouse. Come on. We might be able to move it!'

The two captives proceeded to ransack the two partitions of the vault for means of getting up to the cover in the roof which pointed towards freedom. Splashing through the water, which was now up to Sandra's waist, they pushed a table underneath the trap and placed a box and some chairs upon it. Then Danny stood on them and heaved at the iron cover. For some minutes it resisted his attempt to move it, but at last with a hollow clang it opened, sending a shower of rubble down into the vault. Sandra scrambled up beside Danny, and in a short time the two of them were once again on the firm earth of the street.

'The question is,' Danny said, 'what do we do now?'

'I'm going to go home and change,'

Sandra said. 'That is, if I don't get pneumonia on the way.'

'I've got to get Bronislawski,' Danny said. 'I wish to hell I knew where he's gone. I had that darned paper with all the information on it, but I never looked at it. Your brother was a clever man, Sandra. When he said that information was on his skin, he put us all off the scent. He wore a body belt and he kept the paper in the pocket, right on top of his skin.'

'But I know where Bronislawski has gone,' Sandra said. 'While I was with him in that horrible place he spoke quite freely. The ship with the guns on board is a small fishing boat, and Bronislawski and his gang are meeting her at a place called Marshwood.'

'Marshwood!' Danny exclaimed. 'That's in Essex on the estuary. Look, Sandra, I'm going to ring up the Yard. You'd better go along with the wagon when it arrives. You'll catch your death of cold in those wet clothes.'

The two of them ranged the streets looking for a telephone kiosk. Passers-by looked with wonder at the bedraggled man and woman, but once on the phone Danny lost no time. He was soon talking to the chief.

'Thank the Lord it's you,' the chief said. 'We've been looking for you everywhere.'

'Save that for now,' Danny told him, and went on to explain what had happened. The chief listened intently, and then said,

'I'm sending a launch along. You'd better get aboard with the girl. They'll have some warm things for the pair of you, I expect. But for mercy's sake keep out of trouble now. We'll be down at Marshwood in a few minutes and we'll nab those birds red-handed. And by the way, King, your hunch was right. Bronislawski killed Jones in Mayfair and took the body to where you found it. The gangster lured Jones to his flat on some pretext, and must have shot him just after you saw Jones in the lift. He must have taken the sister down to Jones's place later, with the intention of getting rid of both of them, when he found you there and had to abandon his plan. Too bad you couldn't get the information from Jones, but never mind. This is good work. Keep it up, boy, and don't go looking for trouble. Those thugs of Bronislawski's are dangerous.'

'You're telling me,' Danny said, and hung up.

Soon he and Sandra, dry and warm again, were on the police launch making swift progress downriver.

The inspector captained the craft capably. 'We've got a hustle on,' he explained. 'The tide turns in an hour, and they'll try to finish before it goes down.'

The launch chugged on past the warehouses, yards and factories, until fields and trees began to line the river bank. The salt wind from the sea grew fresher and stronger.

'We should see them soon,' the inspector said. 'I'm going to slow up. They'll hear the engine racing a mile off.' Accordingly, he reduced speed and began to make for the shore. At the same time, the radio man announced that he had made contact with the flying squad cars on the road and with other launches in the river.

'The squad cars have found them, sir,' the radio man reported, 'and they've got the lorries. Apparently there's been a bit of a scramble. The boat that brought 'em the stuff is heading downriver without lights. But the gangsters on land are all nabbed.'

'Good work,' the inspector said. 'We'll get 'em before they reach the three-mile limit.'

They started the motor again when suddenly a policeman on the launch shouted and pointed into the pitch-black night ahead of them. Danny, looking to where he pointed, could just see the shape of a ship's prow bearing down on them. He sprang up in alarm as the inspector shouted commands to the helmsman. The launch spun round, away from the vessel which bore down on them without lights, going full steam ahead. The launch's bows just swung clear in time and the ship glided past. It was a small coaster such as is often seen in the Thames.

But Danny, standing precariously on the launch's slippery deck, was unbalanced by the sudden swing, and toppled outward towards the darkened stranger. As she swung by, he grasped her rail and fell forward upon it. Clinging desperately, he clambered and watched the friendly launch recede into the darkness. He was now on the enemy's own ship, and he took great comfort from the Smith & Wesson revolver in the pocket of the clothes which the police launch had provided.

No one seemed to have heard him come aboard. Behind him, he heard the police launch's engine roaring, while a searchlight's bright beam pierced the night and began to sweep around the water. Before him, Danny could see the vessel's wheelhouse and a faint ray of light shining through hatches over the door and windows. He slipped his gun into his hand and made towards the wheelhouse door. Inside he could hear voices.

'I tell you, Karl, we can't get away from these launches,' said a voice which Danny did not recognize. 'They're too fast for us. Already they're using their searchlights to look for us, and soon they'll start firing.'

'Then get the guns manned and fire back. Have Sven shoot the damn searchlights out,' Bronislawski said. As he spoke, the launch's light found the ship, lighting up Danny as, revolver in hand, he stood outside the wheelhouse door.

He wrenched the door open and went inside.

'Come on,' he told the men inside. 'This is the police. Get 'em up and keep 'em up.'

Bronislawski, who had been talking to four other men who were obviously the officers of the ship, started up with a cry which was checked by the cold glint in Danny's eyes.

'I'm arresting you, Petroff or Bronislawski, for the murder of Sidney Mason,' Danny said.

'Drop that gun, you, and put your hands up,' a voice behind Danny said.

'Shoot, Paul, shoot and kill him,' Bronislawski shouted. 'Get — '

But before he could finish, something struck the ship with a shuddering jar which made all the lights flicker and threw Danny into the wheelhouse. Behind him a pistol roared and the big fat uniformed captain slumped to the ground. Bronislawski sprang up and kicked Danny's revolver, which had fallen from his reach, onto the deck outside; and his hand, at the same time, flashed upwards, a knife in it, wicked and curved, ready to strike.

But Danny was ready for the gangster. Recovering his balance, he struck Bronislawski a haymaker on the chin so that he doubled up and fell just as one of the other men came plunging down on the policeman, whirling his fists. Danny's elbow crashed into the man's body and then he went down, fighting, to the floor of the narrow wheelhouse. Heavy boots trod on his legs. Clumsy blows crunched into his body and then, through his daze, he heard voices shouting. The police from the launch had arrived. The weight on top of him eased and he emerged to find a dozen policemen, all armed, rounding up the crew. The fight was over.

But Bronislawski was not finished yet. Dazed and shaken, he had crawled outside the deckhouse. Through an arch in the bodies of two policemen in front of him, Danny saw the gangster raising his weapon to fire. He charged forward and the revolver went off near his face, smashing past his ear, spraying his head with heat. Then his fists crashed into the gangster's chin and body. He staggered back to the rail where Danny hit him again on the point of the jaw. Bronislawski toppled backwards over the side and disappeared into the murky water.

The ship had not yet stopped, and as he saw the white face of Bronislawski flash by in the water, Danny ran aft. But his enemy had disappeared, drawn under the vessel, and as Danny gazed into the searchlight's beams while they played on the stern, he saw a body tossing and heaving in the white wake of the vessel, a wake that was stained with blood. There could be no doubt as to the gangster's fate in the ship's screws. Danny turned away.

Sandra came running up to him.

'Are you all right, darling?'

'I'm fine now,' Danny said, hugging her. 'For the love of Pete, let's do this sort of thing more privately.' He looked round at the grinning men. 'These policemen have no souls for romance.'

Purposefully, Sandra led him to the shelter of the hatchway . . .

We do hope that you have enjoyed reading this large print book.

Did you know that all of our titles are available for purchase?

We publish a wide range of high quality large print books including:
Romances, Mysteries, Classics
General Fiction
Non Fiction and Westerns

Special interest titles available in large print are:
The Little Oxford Dictionary
Music Book, Song Book
Hymn Book, Service Book

Also available from us courtesy of Oxford University Press:
Young Readers' Dictionary
(large print edition)
Young Readers' Thesaurus
(large print edition)

For further information or a free brochure, please contact us at:
Ulverscroft Large Print Books Ltd.,
The Green, Bradgate Road, Anstey,
Leicester, LE7 7FU, England.
Tel: (00 44) **0116 236 4325**
Fax: (00 44) **0116 234 0205**

FROST LINE

Ardath Mayhar and
Mary Wickizer Burgess

A helpless woman is attacked in her home by a ruthless gang of murderers and thieves searching for her brother's valuable gun collection. They fail in their mission, and now they're coming back to finish the job — this time determined to leave no eye witnesses alive. Sheriff Washington Shipp must use all his instincts and expertise to track them down before they can strike again. But one of the criminals, more dangerous than all the rest, is leaving a trail of bodies across Louisiana — and Wash may be next in line . . .

LORD JAMES HARRINGTON AND THE CHRISTMAS MYSTERY

Lynn Florkiewicz

It's Christmas, and James and Beth are preparing for Harrington's festive dinner and dance. This year, famous diva Olivia Dupree is singing, a wedding is taking place, and they're hosting a reunion of Pals — ex-army comrades from the Great War. When Olivia falls ill and claims she's been poisoned, James puts his sleuthing hat on. But things take a sinister turn when a further attack occurs. What links the two victims? James must race against time to stop multiple murders taking place.

THE FRIGHTENED MAN

Gerald Verner

Samuel Coyne sends his ward Diana to enlist detective Paul Rivington as a bodyguard because three attempts have been made on his life. Although he denies knowing the attacker's motive or identity, he has erected elaborate defences around his house. Paul arranges for his brother and partner Bob to take on the job. Later, Bob captures an intruder on the grounds, who recognises Coyne as somebody he calls Kilroe. Surprisingly, Coyne lets the man go, not wishing to prosecute. Then they discover that Diana has mysteriously disappeared . . .

AMERICAN LEGIONNAIRE

John Robb

Amid the burning sands of the desert, the French Foreign Legion is constructing a new fort at Vateau — deep in the territory of El Dowla, ruthless leader of the Bormones, in constant struggle with France for control of the region. He aims to strike hard at the half-built stronghold before it is finished. Meanwhile, among the legionnaires sent out to protect Vateau is an American named Dice Regan — who has a very personal score to settle with El Dowla . . .

DATA HUNTER

Steven Fox

Robert Moonsinger, internet private investigator, receives visitors from three US government departments. They want him to find out how funds from banks — including the Federal Reserve — and important schematics of a secret military prototype have been stolen, and by whom. A lucrative offer is made, and he agrees to take the case — thus endangering his own life and that of others close to him. For Moonsinger is pitched against a vast criminal organization, headed by an utterly ruthless man for whom murder is the weapon of choice . . .